Delia walked back and forth across the concrete sidewalk for several minutes, waiting to hear the clatter of a screwdriver in the library door. The door lock hadn't worked in years; now, to get it open, it was necessary to persuade it with the tip of a Phillips.

Finally, when her watch showed ten minutes past the hour, Delia pounded on the door again. After waiting a few seconds, she walked around the building with an idea of knocking on the back door. She pressed her face against the windows that ran across the rear of the library office, took a few seconds to convince herself of what she'd seen, and then turned and walked briskly to the police station.

Also by Deborah Adams
Published by Ballantine Books:

ALL THE GREAT PRETENDERS

ALL THE CRAZY WINTERS

Deborah Adams

BALLANTINE BOOKS • NEW YORK

Copyright © 1992 by Deborah Adams

All rights reserved under International and Pan-American Copyright Conventions. Published in the United States of America by Ballantine Books, a division of Random House, Inc., New York, and simultaneously in Canada by Random House of Canada Limited, Toronto.

Library of Congress Catalog Card Number: 91-92391

ISBN 0-345-37076-7

Manufactured in the United States of America

First Edition: July 1992

AUTHOR'S NOTE

I am extremely grateful to
Ethel, Pam, Marilyn, and both Rhondas
for taking the time to show me every potential
weapon in the Humphreys County Public Library.

In memory of James Proctor,
the last true Southern gentleman

CHAPTER
1

DELIA CANNON WAS ON HER WAY HOME from the Thanksgiving visit with her daughter when she noticed the fire. Sparks were shooting up into the clear autumn night like a display of miniature but enthusiastic fireworks. So even while Delia was still miles away from the source, she could see the flames.

Delia had never been a woman to seek out disaster. She never poked past the scene of an accident, sneaking glances into the remains of whatever vehicle had been involved. When sirens screamed past her house, she didn't even peek out the window to determine whether the emergency involved police or ambulance. The reason she speeded up now was simply that, having lived in Jesus Creek all her life, she knew everyone in town. Whatever had happened was going to affect her in some way.

As Delia passed the city limits sign (WELCOME TO JESUS CREEK, POP. 430) she could see that it was the Host house, one of the oldest in town. A line of cars

1

was parked along both sides of Highway 70 just east
of town and people were standing beside their cars,
staring in amazed silence at the flames. Jesus
Creek's only fire engine was parked in the Host
front yard, along with a patrol car and the private
vehicles belonging to members of the community's
volunteer fire department. Delia cruised along until she found an open space between a Volkswagen
and Frankie Mae Weathers's station wagon, then
pulled in between them.

As Delia made her way through the milling crowd
and the scurrying officials one section of the roof
caved in as if in slow motion. Spectators and firemen backed away without taking their eyes off the
flame-encased house.

"Frankie Mae!" Delia called, coming up to the
older woman. Frankie Mae was wearing her pith
helmet, one of the little whimsies that caused some
people to wonder about her. "What happened? Is
Oliver okay?"

Frankie Mae nodded. "He's around here somewhere. You can't miss him. Wearing a velvet
housecoat with his big old white legs sticking out
of it."

"My God, this is awful!" Delia said, turning back
to the conflagration. The Host family had lived in
that house for over a century and a half. It wasn't
the first one erected in Jesus Creek, but old Edward
Host came in a close second. He'd built this beauty
himself, every wall and floor, and built it to last.
Now it was nothing but a few black beams exposed
by the ravenous flame.

"Roger with you?" Frankie Mae asked suddenly.

"No," Delia told her. "I've been in Nashville,
having dinner with Charlotte and Al."

Frankie Mae nodded solemnly. She knew that a visit with Charlotte and the new husband could put Delia off for days afterward. "She still married to that train fella?"

"Engineer," Delia corrected. "Al's a chemical engineer. And yes, they're still married."

"Here comes Reb," Frankie Mae said. "You wanna run? I'll head him off."

"Thanks for the offer," Delia said. "But I think I can handle him. Reb hasn't been a danger since he stopped putting lizards down my shirt."

Frankie Mae shrugged, as if she couldn't imagine why Delia would consider herself any safer now that Reb carried a gun instead of reptiles.

Police chief Reb Gassler was striding toward them—toward Delia, actually—looking chipper despite the sweat stains on his shirt and the smudged soot on his face. "Hello, Delia. You out by yourself?"

Delia looked around. "Seems like I'm out with the whole town. Frankie Mae says Oliver is okay."

"Not exactly. He keeps trying to run into the fire to get his documents. I haven't figured out yet which documents he means."

"Family research," the two women said together.

Reb looked at them as if they were speaking gibberish. "Why?" he asked.

"Reb, he's got—or he had—the finest, most extensive collection of genealogical data in the state. Lord! I hadn't even thought of that. What a terrible waste."

"Is it worth his life?" Reb asked.

Delia didn't try to explain. Reb wasn't interested in genealogy. He didn't understand the thrill of holding in your hands a letter written two hundred years ago or the exhilaration of finding a name, a date, a marriage record that had eluded you for decades. If Delia had said that she sympathized with Oliver's attempts to risk going through fire to rescue his research, Reb would have thought she'd lost her mind.

"Do you have any idea how the fire started?" she asked him.

"Nothing official," Reb said cautiously, then shrugged. "It's arson."

"Arson!" Frankie Mae exclaimed. "Shoot, you're just looking for attention. Who'd set fire to Oliver's house?"

Delia could tell that she and Reb were thinking the same thing—that almost anyone in town would rejoice to see Oliver burned at the stake. But they were both too discreet to articulate the sentiment right there in Oliver's yard with his house plummeting before their eyes.

"There's a gas can over there," Reb said, pointing toward the patrol car and one of the other policemen. "We found it in the yard. Oliver says it's not his. We won't know for sure until the fire chief can get in there, but it looks like it started in Oliver's library."

"Where Oliver kept all his genealogical material," Delia said.

"Those old papers burn quick." Reb turned back toward the house. The wall fragments were collapsing faster now. The firemen had abandoned hope of saving the structure; they were merely hosing down the grass and trees. "Good thing we've had plenty rainfall this year. I tell you, Delia, if you ever want to torch a house, be sure to pour the gasoline close to a heater or a stove. Don't be as stupid as the nutcase who did this."

Delia stood watching the flames eat their way through the old home. She almost imagined the spirits of Oliver's ancestors floating up into the night sky, along with the ashes of a lifetime of research.

The crowd had grown quieter as the blazing house settled to the ground. A cold wind had started up, sending a few of the spectators to their cars for jackets and gloves, but the firemen seemed to have matters under control. Delia pulled her own coat around her a little tighter and stood silently watching the once solid house dissolve into ash and smoke.

CHAPTER
2

DELIA ARRIVED AT THE JESUS CREEK PUB-
lic Library five minutes before opening time and
knocked on the glass door at the front of the building. When no one responded, she leaned against the
brick to wait. If Pamela was working, the door
would open at exactly ten o'clock. But today was
Pamela's day off, and only head librarian Estelle
Carhart and one of the volunteers would be in. It
might be a while before anyone remembered to un-
lock the door.

The chill wind that had started Saturday night
was still blowing strong, and Delia could feel it bit-
ing into her exposed cheeks. She should have worn
a heavier coat, but her daily speed walk (five times
around the court square) was easier with lighter
garments. She'd hoped the temperature would
climb a bit before the day waned, but obviously op-
timism was not going to help. Jesus Creek, Tennessee did not normally experience winter, unless you
counted the drizzle that passed for rain during most

of February. This sudden cold snap had already taken its toll on Delia's poor old bones. Not that she was old, of course. Forty-six was barely middle age, depending on your definition. But certainly something had been happening to her body these past few years. And then there was that god-awful calendar that rolled over faster and faster every month. Reluctantly she was forced to admit that she had vivid firsthand recollections of many of the events that were now being taught in high-school history classes.

Delia's depressing reverie was interrupted by the sight of Miss Constance Winter. The old woman was scurrying past, her bright orange plaid coat standing out boldly against the gray morning.

"Hello, Miss Constance!" Delia called.

Miss Constance came to an abrupt stop, the upper half of her body leaning forward as she peered around her to see who'd called. Constance Winter was the last in a long line of Winters, each one of them unique. Or as some people chose to call them, just plain nuts. Constance carried on the family tradition. Her particular form of battiness exhibited itself just the way Delia was now observing. Bright and early every morning, Miss Constance would arrive in downtown Jesus Creek, dressed in whatever clothes she'd thrown on and bearing home-baked goodies. She proceeded to enter every business in town, offering cookies or candy and stopping to chat with anyone willing to listen to her stream-of-consciousness recitation on the weather, crops, family, and national current events. (The latter Miss Constance gleaned from her favorite tabloid.)

Carrying a nine-by-thirteen-inch baking pan to-

day, she couldn't spare a hand to wave, so she nodded. "Delia," she said briskly. "Likely to catch bron-
ichal pneumony out here in this weather."

"What about you?" Delia asked, even though
she'd stopped worrying about Miss Constance's
health years ago. No matter how old the woman got
or how inappropriately she might be dressed, Miss
Constance Winter had never been known to develop so much as the sniffles. Bronchial pneumonia
was definitely out of the question.

"I got my remedies to help me," Miss Constance
assured her. "Got to git before the coal burns out.
Have one, will you?" Miss Constance offered up her
baking pan.

"Thank you, no" Delia said. "I'm going into the
library just as soon as it opens, and I can't carry
food in there." Technically, Delia was telling the
truth. There really was a rule against eating in the
library, but Delia observed it no more than did anyone else. The truth was she refused a brownie because she didn't trust Miss Constance's impromptu
recipes.

"Well, then," Miss Constance said, and skittered
away.

Delia walked back and forth across the concrete
sidewalk for several minutes, waiting to hear the
clatter of a screwdriver in the door. The door lock
hadn't worked in years; now, to get it open, it was
necessary to persuade it with the tip of a Phillips.

Finally, when her watch showed ten minutes past
the hour, Delia pounded on the door again. After
waiting a few seconds, she walked around the
building with an idea of knocking on the back door.
She pressed her face against the windows that ran
across the rear of the library office, took a few sec-

onds to convince herself of what she'd seen, then turned and walked briskly to the police station.

Police chief Reb Gassler and deputy chief German Hunt refused to allow Delia inside what they referred to as the scene of the crime. Being a woman of great curiosity, limited patience, and quiet cunning, Delia simply followed them in and planted herself firmly in a corner of the vandalized office. Books and papers were strewn everywhere, an old Underwood typewriter lay on its side on the floor, and pieces of glass from a broken coffeepot glittered in the corner.

German looked up from his work. "Better not touch anything," he warned.

"Of course not," said Delia. "Where on earth do you suppose Estelle is? Could she have gone to report the break-in?"

"She'da just called, wouldn't she?" Reb pointed out. "What time does this place open?"

"Ten A.M." Delia answered. "If Pamela is here, that is; but this is her day off. Estelle is a little more casual about opening time."

"Better give Estelle a call at home and have her come on down," Reb instructed his deputy.

German nodded, picked up the phone, and dialed information. It could take hours to find a phone book in the jumble of papers and books.

"You'd better call Pamela, too," Delia said. "She'll probably be able to tell us what's missing better than Estelle could." Turning to Reb, she asked, "What do you suppose this is all about? Why would anyone break into a library?"

Reb pointed to an empty metal box that had been tossed on the floor. "Cash box. Probably some dopie

looking for money. That or just some kids express-
ing their displeasure with parental restrictions."

Delia looked closely at Chief Reb. She'd never
heard him use so many polysyllabic words.

"They talked about that at the seminar last
week." Reb gave her a sheepish grin.

"Mrs. Carhart doesn't answer. Why don't I go
ahead and call Pamela?" German still had the receiver in his hand.

"Fine, fine," Reb said, pulling out his pocket
notepad. "Now, Delia. Tell me what happened when
you first got here."

"Very simply, I arrived a little before ten. I'm a
Friend of the Library, you see, and once a week I
come in to do volunteer work. Typing or telephon-
ing people who've failed to return books or whatever needs doing. At the moment I'm transferring
the census records on microfilm into an alphabetical file."

"You always come on Monday?"

"Almost always. We have a schedule. You can
probably find it in here somewhere, with all the
volunteers listed and the days they're supposed to
work."

"They all do the same thing you do?"

"Pretty much. Except for the genealogical record.
That's my specialty. Alphabetizing the census
makes it a lot easier for researchers."

"Uh-huh," Reb commented uncertainly. He didn't
ask for an elaboration.

"Since the door was locked, I assumed that Estelle had just forgotten to open up. I went around
back, found the door open and the office looking a
mess, and then I walked up to the police station to
tell you."

"And you didn't see anyone hanging around?"

"No one at all," Delia assured him.

"Pamela will be here in a few minutes," German told them after he'd replaced the receiver. "Said she didn't have any idea where Mrs. Carhart could be."

"I imagine she'll be along soon," Delia put in. "Estelle may be late sometimes, but she never fails to open up. Anyway, one of the volunteers should have been here by now."

"Right." Reb looked at his watch. "German, why don't you hightail it on over to Estelle's house and see if you can rouse her." Estelle lived just a few hundred feet behind the library in one of the nicer Victorians. "Delia, you don't have to stay. We'll take care of things."

"Thank you, Reb, but I'd better wait for Pamela. She's going to need some help cleaning this mess. Do you suppose I should call the other Friends?"

Reb shrugged. "Don't guess it matters."

"Fingerprints," German reminded him. The deputy was a zealous cop, always keenly aware of the possibility of a major crime wave. He'd almost had his moment of glory last summer, while Reb was away on vacation. Unfortunately, German had been upstaged by a visiting psychic who'd solved the case right under the deputy's nose.

"Oh, hell. Why don't you take care of that after you get Estelle, German?" Chief Reb settled himself into a corner and sighed. "It's always something. Man can't even take a break anymore."

German threw his chief an exasperated glance and left by the back door, stopping just outside to rid himself of a wad of Red Man.

Reb grinned at Delia. "Boy's a hot dog. You got

any idea how many fingerprints there'll be in here?"

"Still," Delia said, "it's good to see a young man show enthusiasm for his job."

"I suppose," Reb said grudgingly. "I guess even I might have been pretty gung ho once upon a time."

"I suppose you might have been." Delia gave him a cautious smile. Reb had been half-smitten with Delia since grammar school. Neither her marriage nor his had stopped his wistful glances. Now that both of them were divorced, Reb seemed to have accelerated his campaign, but Delia knew—and she suspected Reb did, too—that their relationship was never meant to be more than friendly.

"As long as you're here, I might as well give you the third degree. Did you notice anything out of place?"

Delia looked around the vandalized room and decided he meant objects other than strewn books and garbage. There was an old kitchen counter along one wall. Normally it held a coffeepot and a small microwave oven plus a half-dozen containers of cookies, breads, chips, and other munchies. Now all those things except the microwave lay broken on the floor. The worktable in the middle of the room was cleared of the books and papers usually piled on it. They were on the floor along with the rickety Underwood manual that Pamela often used.

The remaining two walls had floor-to-ceiling bookshelves that usually held more newspapers and shoes than books. Those were only partially empty, as if the vandal had grown tired halfway through the rampage.

Worst of all, a trash bag had been split open,

spilling some very old fruit and the remains of one of Estelle's frozen diet meals across the floor. The air was ripe with the odor of all that, plus something else Delia couldn't identify.

"The only obvious thing, I guess, is the key. Why is it in the door? And who does it belong to? Or, to whom does it belong?" Delia, an early retiree from the Angela County Public School System, had taught fourth grade for over twenty years. Even now she felt the need for grammatical vigilance.

"Has to be Estelle's," Reb said, pointing to the large, macramé key ring. "She must have come in this morning, opened up, seen all this mess, and gone to report it. I'm surprised we didn't meet her on the way, though."

"Well, that could be. Maybe she did the sensible thing, for a change. You know, getting the hell out of the way in case the burglar was still in here."

Reb didn't seem convinced.

German returned with his crime kit tucked under one arm. "Estelle's not home," he said breathlessly. Obviously he'd been running, hurrying to return to the library before he missed anything. "I'll try to get this finished before Pamela gets here."

Delia had been aware of German's presence around the library these past few weeks. More specifically, she'd noticed his presence around Pamela. He seemed to have a bad case of infatuation. So far, Pamela didn't seem to have noticed, but Delia suspected it wouldn't be long before German revved up his pursuit.

He'd barely begun his work when Pamela did, indeed, arrive. German had told her to come through the front door so he could prepare her for the shock. Pamela came through the back.

Impeccably dressed, as usual, in a narrow skirt and hand-knitted sweater, Pamela surveyed the room quickly, taking in everyone and everything. The sight of destroyed equipment and mistreated books stunned her. "My God!" she cried, and reached for the counter to steady herself.

"Ah, Pamela," German said. Putting his kit on the desk, he set up a chair that had been over-turned on the floor and guided her to it. "You're not gonna faint, are you? Sit here and calm down."

"All right, German," Chief Reb said gruffly. "Stop baby-sitting and get on with it."

German gave Pamela's shoulder one last tender pat and quickly began unpacking his equipment. He knew as well as anyone that it was a hopeless task since Estelle Carhart's office usually resembled the scene of a tea party. Everyone who used the library on anything like a regular basis also used the office for coffee, lunch, and bathroom facilities.

"When will we be able to start cleaning up?" Delia asked. "I'd hate for Estelle to come in and find this . . . chaos."

Reb shrugged. "Guess I'd better get the Polaroid and take a picture or two. German, go get the camera."

German sighed and carefully put down his kit, then left to get the official police camera.

Reb leaned against the wall and watched his deputy go. "No point having a deputy if you can't use him for the dirty work." He grinned at the two women.

"Pamela," Delia asked, "do you have any idea where Estelle could be?"

Pamela Satterfield looked at her dainty gold watch and frowned. "Almost eleven. Estelle should have been here by nine to get ready for opening."

"Reckon *she* could have done this?" Reb asked.

Pamela shook her head. "Of course not. Why would anyone do this? It's disgusting! Just look at these books, thrown around, stepped on—"

"Did these books come from the shelves out front?" Delia asked. "It doesn't look as if anything out there has been touched."

"No, these haven't been processed yet. We're always backlogged. If the board would see fit to provide us with a computer, everything would run much smoother."

Reb checked his watch and frowned. "All right. Let's get ahold of Estelle and wrap this up before lunch time."

The complete investigation took only minutes, since Reb refused to let German do more than the minimal amount of work. After collecting a few fingerprints and photographing the room, Reb pulled his deputy out the back door and left instructions for Delia: "Holler if you find anything unusual." With the officials out of the way, Pamela could begin the tedious job of straightening and cleaning. Grabbing sheets of paper from the floor, she smoothed the creases out with her palm—trembling with shock and fury as she did so—and stacked them in haphazard piles on the worktable.

"Maybe I should put a note on the door, explaining that the library will be closed for the day," Delia suggested.

Pamela nodded miserably and reached for another handful of papers. "It will take the whole day to get this cleaned up and then we'll be even more behind than usual. What sort of demented . . . ?"

"Look on the bright side, Pamela. At least the main reading room is untouched."

"It looks okay. But we can't be certain until we've done a complete inventory."

Delia nodded. "I suppose there might be some books missing. But why on earth would anyone steal library books?"

"Happens all the time," Pamela assured her. "Some people just get a kick out of stealing. Absolutely no respect for books or rules and no respect for the library. They don't appreciate the luxury of being able to come in here and read. . . ." Pamela smiled weakly. "Sorry. But I get so angry about the carelessness and neglect. And frankly, Delia, the board is no better than the thieves. They refuse to part with money to run this place properly. They would, you know, if Eliza Leach told them to, but she could care less. Last year they approved a small fortune for purchasing chairs in the main room, but you can forget about a computer or books or—"

"I'll stick this on the door," Delia said, holding up the note she'd written. "And then I'll try calling Estelle again. I can't imagine why she isn't in yet. German went to her house, but she wasn't there."

"You know Estelle," Pamela said. "She probably decided to go shopping. And where is Marilyn? She was supposed to fill in for me today. What about Walt Jr.?"

"No one's seen Marilyn, either. I'll give her a call at home. What *about* Walt Jr.?" Walt was Estelle's son, the spitting image of his father, except for his sexual preference. That was something Delia had stumbled upon quite innocently one day outside a Nashville restaurant. Walt had been putting his— ah, friend—into a car, saying goodbye with a quick peck on the cheek. Walt Jr. hadn't seen Delia, and she hadn't mentioned it to him. But Delia was certain that Estelle had no idea, else why would she keep talking about her son's finding some nice girl and settling down?

"Walt Jr. was visiting Estelle this weekend. At least, Estelle said on Friday that she was expecting him. Wasn't he there, either?"

"I don't think so. German didn't mention it. Probably Walt Jr. went back to Nashville. Doesn't he have to work today?"

Pamela shrugged to indicate that young Mr. Carhart's schedule was no concern of hers.

In the library proper Delia taped the note to the outside door, then settled herself behind the desk to use the phone. If Estelle didn't answer, maybe she'd call some of the librarian's neighbors. Lax as Estelle was about business, Delia couldn't believe she'd simply forget to come to work.

She phoned Marilyn first and got an answer right away. "Oh, Delia," Marilyn said breathlessly. "I was going to call Estelle in just a few minutes. I can't make it in today. Jamie's got a dreadful stomach virus and I really can't see leaving him with a sitter. Thank goodness you're there. You can give Estelle a hand."

"Actually, Marilyn, Estelle hasn't arrived yet. You haven't heard from her?"

"Not me," Marilyn said. "But you might try calling—oh, Jamie's throwing up again. You'll have to excuse me, Delia." And Marilyn hung up.

Delia sighed and wondered who Marilyn had

meant to suggest as a helping hand. Perhaps, if Estelle didn't turn up soon, she'd call Marilyn back and ask.

From the back room came a crash and Pamela's startled cry of disgust.

Delia found her standing over the pile of shattered glass, hands pressed to her mouth. "I dropped it," she mumbled. "I was going to pick up the pieces of this broken coffeepot and I wound up just dumping all of it right back on the floor."

"Pamela, sit down here and take deep breaths. This really isn't so bad. We'll get the books and papers put away, I'll clean up all the glass, and then everything will be back to normal." Delia sounded like a patient mother trying to appease a hyperactive child.

Pamela eased herself into a chair.

"Do you keep the broom in here?" Delia pulled open a closet door.

The broom was inside. So was a dustpan. And several bottles of cleansers. All of them were piled haphazardly atop the body of Estelle Carhart.

CHAPTER
3

REB AND GERMAN HAD RESPONDED IN REC-
ord time to Delia's frantic phone call. After questioning Delia (it wasn't possible to question poor,
hysterical Pamela, they'd decided) German offered
to drive both women home. Ordinarily Delia would
have argued and insisted that she be allowed to stay
and witness whatever investigation Reb planned to
pursue, but for once, the challenge of a new experience had not appealed to her.

Delia walked the half mile or so home. She'd lived
in Jesus Creek all her life. In junior high and senior high, she'd hung out with the gang at Eloise's
Diner on Main Street. She'd circled the square with
her new husband, trailing shoes and tin cans behind the car. Later she'd pushed Charlotte in her
stroller along these sidewalks. And for the last two
years she'd been taking her daily walk around the
court square. Downtown Jesus Creek and the people who worked and shopped there were as comfortable as her own bedroom. Or had been until

today. The town looked different to her now, as if all the familiar houses and roads had been stripped away and replaced by some alien community full of dangerous strangers.

The phone was ringing when Delia let herself into her small frame house on Morning Glory Way. She dropped her purse onto a nearby chair and slipped off her shoes before picking up the receiver.

"Dee? You sound out of breath." The familiar voice belonged to Roger Shelton.

"I am, Roger. I've just walked back from the library and I suppose I was going faster than my regular pace. Roger, Estelle Carhart is dead."

"You're kidding." Roger paused, waiting for the punch line.

"No, I'm not. We found her in the closet."

"What was she doing in the closet?"

"We don't know. She was sort of folded up in there, and all the paraphernalia from the shelves—cleansers and such—had fallen on top of her." Delia was working hard to keep her voice firm and steady, but apparently she wasn't fooling Roger any more than herself.

"I assume you're upset. Need company?"

"Maybe later. Let me get myself cleaned up and settled down. You wouldn't believe how unpleasant a dead body can be. Or how dirty it can make the rest of us feel. I just want to get in the tub and scrub straight through to the bone." In fact, Delia had just noticed that she was holding the receiver gingerly between her thumb and forefinger so as not to transfer any more of the library atmosphere to her home than necessary.

"Go ahead. I'll be there in an hour or so and I'll fix dinner. Anything special you'd like?"

"Frankly, Roger, I don't plan to eat ever again."

"I know. That'll change by the time you calm down. Trust me. Just take it easy for a little while, Dee. I'll be there as soon as I can."

Delia replaced the phone and started for the bathroom, unbuttoning her blouse as she went. She paused in the hallway, then retraced her steps and carefully locked the front door.

At her age, of course, she'd experienced the deaths of several friends and family members. It's just that they'd all been dead in the funeral home, all tidied and spruced up and . . . prepared. Looking at Estelle's fresh (or relatively so) corpse had left Delia feeling raw. She wanted more than anything to climb into the bathtub and close herself in until that inexplicable feeling of embarrassment went away.

With the water running and her clothes in a heap on the cool tile floor, Delia eased herself into the bubbles. Lavender scent. She'd heard that it relieved depression, and while she wasn't exactly feeling depressed, that came close enough to describing her current disposition. Anger, perhaps. And guilt—guilt that she had not done something to prevent the death of a dear friend.

Death shouldn't have been a terror for Estelle, that soft, vague woman with an accent of the Old South. It should have come sweetly in the middle of a magnolia-scented night.

Estelle had never really lived in the same world with the rest of them, never lived in that world where violence and cruelty were abundant. When they were children, Estelle never got into fights or even climbed trees. Her idea of fun had been to have a tea party, a real tea party with her mother's good service, or to dress in the old hoop skirts she'd found in the attic. Estelle could keep up the performance all day, even after her playmates had wandered away to play tag.

Tears trickled down Delia's cheeks and her chest began to heave as the sobbing grew stronger. Even Delia wasn't certain if she was weeping for Estelle or for her own frightened self.

Roger arrived loaded with provisions. Pizza for two, a bottle of wine, a handful of flowers, and a half-dozen Goo Goos.

"If the wine doesn't help, we can resort to chocolate," he said cheerfully. "Do we eat in the living room or go whole hog and spread out the good china?"

"Living room," Delia said, wrapping her bathrobe around her and jerking the belt tight. "Just dump all that stuff from the coffee table onto the floor and we'll eat the pizza from the box. I will insist on glasses for the wine, however."

"We'd feel jollier if we slugged it straight from the bottle."

"No doubt. But jolly isn't what I'm after tonight."

Roger cleared a space on the table, then tore the top off the box and separated two pieces of pepperoni-mushroom from his half of the pizza. He stuffed the flowers into an empty pencil holder that he'd found on the bookcase and he placed it beside the pizza. The chocolate he slid under the table.

"Here you go," Delia said, returning from the kitchen with the glasses. "Finest crystal. And how was your visit with the kids?"

"Warm, homey, all that stuff. Elinor is almost the

cook her mother was, and she's beginning to show it around her hips, too. She calls it baby fat—"

"And it probably is," Delia said. "How old is the baby? Two months?"

"Exactly," Roger said. "I have new pictures. Want to see them?" He reached into his back pocket for the wallet that always contained a half-dozen recent photos of his only grandchild.

Delia took the wallet and made appropriate oohing sounds. In truth, the child looked like every other baby in the Western world, but Delia tried to keep her comments to herself. She feared that someday Charlotte would present her with equally average grandchildren and then Roger would surely retaliate.

"Assuming I can manage this," Roger said, struggling to fold his legs underneath the coffee table, "who is going to unwrap me after we've eaten?"

"Nonsense, dear," Delia told him, settling gracefully onto the floor beside him, "we'll just roll you across the room and use you as a doorstop."

"Ouch! Damn! Can't I just sit on the couch and lean across my food?"

"Roger, how difficult can it be if every little old man in Japan eats on the floor?"

"I think you've hit on something there. How many Japanese men do you know who are over six feet tall? If I were shorter, like some very inconsiderate people"—he glanced meaningfully at Delia—"this would be a snap."

"Height has nothing to do with it. You spend too much time sitting at your workbench. Try yoga for a change. Or anything physical."

Roger rolled his eyes. "You can make suggestions like that to a man in my position?" He finally managed to seat himself in something like a tailor's position, but Delia had to admit he did look uncomfortable.

"Oh, Roger. For Pete's sake, sit on the couch and lean over. Here, I'll help."

"You know," he said, rubbing his right leg to relieve the cramp that had already settled in it, "perhaps Estelle has gotten the best end of it, after all. At least she won't get as old as I am."

"Trust me," Delia assured him. "Estelle would have preferred stiff bones."

"So." Roger stretched his long legs out in front of him and leaned back on the sofa, cupping a pizza slice in one hand. "Are you coping with this?"

"With her death? No. It's always a shock to be confronted with mortality. But to find someone . . . God, I never imagined it could be like that."

"It's never pleasant," Roger agreed quietly. He was waiting for her to start talking. He knew she would.

Delia picked a stray slice of pepperoni off her half of the pizza and placed it on the corner of the box.

Roger shook his head. "I've always suspected that you radical vegetarians sneak out by dark of moon and consume vast quantities of raw meat."

"Uh-huh," Delia said. A string of cheese ran from her mouth to the pizza in her hand. After disconnecting it and stuffing most of it in her mouth, she added, "And sometimes we rip the flesh from those who antagonize us."

Roger stuck out his tongue.

"I realize it's never pleasant," she said after a moment's consideration. "Maybe I'm more upset, though, because of the irrationality of this particular death. Being an intelligent, reasonable woman,

I should be able to accept it, shouldn't I? No matter how or when it comes, death is still just a piece in the big puzzle. So why have I spent my life avoiding funerals and hospitals and, for that matter, grief in any form?"

"You want my opinion or would you rather work this out for yourself?"

Delia looked up at him and shrugged. "I found the vandalism first," she said at last. "You wouldn't believe the chaos! Why on earth would anyone do that?"

"A struggle?" Roger suggested, then reached for another slice of pizza.

"I don't think so. It looked like someone had just grabbed everything and thrown it on the floor. Of course, at that point we had no idea Estelle was dead. What on earth could she have been doing there in the middle of the night?"

"Why does it have to be middle of the night?"

Delia chose another piece of pizza for herself before answering. "Estelle was in her nightgown and robe. She certainly wouldn't have been dressed that way in the daytime. And her keys were still in the door. Don't you think that's odd?"

"Was Pamela there?"

"No," Delia said. "Not at first. This is Pamela's day off. But we called her when we couldn't find Estelle. Pamela was not a happy puppy when she saw how the office had been wrecked. You know how she is."

"Neurotic," Roger said, nodding.

"Neat," Delia corrected, although he was probably right. "I whipped open the closet door to get a broom and there was Estelle." Now it sounded funny. It hadn't been.

"The first explanation that comes to mind," Roger said, "is that someone wanted a book. Does the library have any rare volumes? Anything worth a lot of money?"

Delia shook her head. "I wouldn't think so. Besides, if someone wanted to steal a book, why not just check it out and never return it, the way everyone else does?"

"That could run into some money, couldn't it? What's the fine these days for overdue books?"

"Nickel a day. But if you never bring it back, it's a moot point. People steal books all the time."

"Okay." Roger took another pizza wedge from the box and chewed slowly while he tried to concoct another explanation. "My next thought would be money itself. Much there?"

"Don't be silly."

"Then that leaves us with only one logical conclusion." Roger sat back, smiling smugly, and waited for Delia to ask.

"Oh really, Sherlock? And what conclusion is that?"

"Someone broke in especially to kill Estelle."

"Right back to my original question: why would Estelle be there in the middle of the night? Wait, don't tell me. You think she received an anonymous note that asked her to meet the killer by the dark of the moon?"

"Do you have a better idea?"

"Not at the moment. I'm still in shock," Delia said. "You can't expect me to think straight. And I'm about to get very drunk, so don't expect my logic to improve." She finished the last drop of wine in her glass and poured more.

"Wonderful! A golden opportunity for me. Would you like to play doctor, little girl?"

"You're much too old for that stratagem, Roger," Delia said.

Roger slid off the sofa and joined Delia on the floor, slipping his arm around her shoulders. "I could just stay here like this and hand you tissues from time to time."

Delia found that she couldn't speak. One thing about Roger: in the four months they'd known each other, his timing was always impeccable. He could almost always tell five seconds before it happened that Delia was about to cry.

CHAPTER

4

IN A SMALL TOWN, MURDER IS NEWS. WHEN it happens, almost everyone is affected because almost everyone is acquainted with the victim.

By nine A.M. Tuesday morning Delia had received five phone calls from people who wanted to impart the bad news before someone else did. When the first call came, she interrupted the long and wonderfully creative tale to explain that *she* had been at the murder site. *She* had discovered Estelle's corpse. *She* knew how it had happened. That tactic blew up in her face. It took a few minutes, but when Delia finally realized she was being pumped for information, she terminated the conversation with a story about burning biscuits.

Never let it be said, she thought, that I don't learn from my mistakes. The next four calls were cut short with the same biscuit ruse. After that she decided to unplug the phone, a drastic measure for her. Delia knew that a monumental crisis only she could thwart would occur the minute she was out of reach.

For breakfast, coffee was all she could handle. She'd given up cigarettes. She would not sacrifice caffeine, not even for health. While it brewed she sat at the table, wrapped in a furry robe and thick socks, and tried to remember something, some vital clue that would point directly to Estelle's killer.

The keys had been in the back door and they had definitely been Estelle's. No one else could possibly have a key ring that large or that full of (probably worthless) keys.

Delia and Reb and German had noticed the broken door glass in passing, but they hadn't paid much attention to it until after Estelle's body was discovered. Reb maintained that the glass had been broken from the outside. What none of them had been able to figure out was why Estelle hadn't noticed it and gone directly to a phone to summon the police, instead of sticking her keys in the door and walking inside. It was possible that she'd tried the lock before she'd noticed the glass, of course, and had been frightened or flustered or both.

If that were true, then Estelle must have seen something from her house, which stood only a few yards behind the library, and gone padding across the parking lot in her robe and slippers. Again, there seemed no sensible reason for her to have done that. But Estelle had not been the most clear-headed of people, and, Delia reasoned, in the middle of the night her logic might have been further obscured by sleep or a sleeping pill or who knew what.

Delia tried to imagine Estelle wandering out of her house and across the alley to the back door of the library, dressed in baby-doll pajamas and slippers, but she kept getting pictures of Ethel Mertz instead of Estelle Carhart. It figured. Back in grammar school, Estelle had established herself early on as the dumb one. Margaret Matthews, the pretty one, had married air force and left Jesus Creek years ago; Margaret had probably found herself another reputation by now. But Eliza Wilson Leach, the ambitious one, and Delia, the smart one, had stayed in Jesus Creek along with Estelle. None of them had been able to outgrow those early labels.

At any rate, now that Delia reflected on it, dying in her jammies was in character for Estelle. She was the sort of woman who went shopping for shoes and brought home milk; she lost her car in the parking lot and, having found it with the help of store employees, drove in the wrong lane to get home. The joy and the frustration of Estelle was that she never noticed how befuddled she was.

Delia poured coffee into her favorite mug and blew on it, absently noting the temperature on the outdoor thermometer and the level of food in the bird feeder. If Estelle had seen something unusual at the library, why hadn't she alerted the police? She'd phoned them often enough in the past—for everything from peculiar lights in the sky to dogs fighting in her yard. Was it possible, Delia wondered, that she'd gone to the library for some reason other than the intruder? Or might she have arrived there first and found herself trapped when the burglar came in?

After the second cup of coffee, Delia managed to get herself dressed and bundled into her layers for walking. Ordinarily she enjoyed those morning constitutionals, although it felt like cheating when exercise was fun. She never planned a route, just let her feet take her anywhere after her self-imposed five times around the courthouse square, and she tried to think pure and enlightening thoughts along the way. This blustery morning she wasn't surprised to find herself making a beeline for the library.

She could see lights on in the front, although there was still a sign on the door explaining that the library was closed until further notice. Delia pressed her face against the glass and peeked in. Sure enough, Pamela Satterfield was there.

Delia tapped on the door to get Pamela's attention. The assistant librarian didn't seem at all surprised to see Delia. Pamela walked briskly to the door, holding the requisite screwdriver in her hand.

"Delia, how good of you to come. I couldn't stand all this clutter, so I thought: well, why not go ahead and get it cleaned up? After all, we can't reopen until everything's organized. And we'll have to do a proper inventory, too. Estelle never got around to that in the all the years I've been here."

"Pamela, I don't think you should fret about that just now," Delia cautioned her. "You're certainly under enough stress without tackling a project that size." It seemed almost as cold inside as it had been out. Delia wondered if Pamela, notorious for her thrift, had cut off the heat to save money.

"Believe me, I'll feel much better once we determine that nothing's missing. I just can't help feeling that the burglar took something, although for the life of me I can't imagine what."

"Yes, Roger and I had the same discussion last

night. Is there a rare book or something of value
that a thief might want?"

"Not that I know of. Then again, as I said, Estelle hasn't done inventory in years. Also I suspect,
you know, that not all the books were properly processed. Terrible as it sounds, Delia, I think Estelle
may have been placing them on the shelves without doing the paperwork."

"Wouldn't you have noticed that before now?"

Pamela rolled her eyes. "I can't keep an eye on
every book in the place, and goodness knows what's
been stolen right out from under us. One day I
caught Estelle telling a patron to just take a book
on home and not to worry about checking it out. It
seems the lady had forgotten her library card. Of
course, she's been with us for years and we've never
had any trouble from her, but you never know. No
sense putting temptation right in her path, is
there?"

"Absolutely not." Delia agreed. She did think,
however, that perhaps Pamela took the books and
the library a bit too seriously. "I'd be glad to help
with the inventory, if you need me."

"In fact, I do. There's the volunteer help, but they
all seem to have emergencies. After Marilyn failed
to show up yesterday—and look where that got us—
this morning I called to ask if she'd give me a hand
cleaning, and she claims she's far too upset to work
here again. Said the place gives her the creeps.
Well, imagine how I feel, I told her."

"Some people don't deal well with tragedy, Pamela. I'll start calling the Friends, and we'll get you
some volunteers until the board hires someone full-
time."

"Hires someone?" Pamela asked.

"Of course. I realize we're all disturbed just now and we're going to miss Estelle dreadfully. We'll never be able to replace her, but, well, it will take more than just you to run this place, won't it?"

"Yes, it will. I hadn't been thinking clearly or I'd have realized that. I suppose the board will want my opinion about whom to hire. I'd better give that some consideration."

"In the meantime I'll give you a hand. When had you planned to start the inventory?"

"Today. I'm almost finished with the office and I see no reason to put this off any longer. If we work steadily, we can be open again by Thursday morning. Just come on along. I'll be ready by the time you've called the other volunteers." Pamela started for the card catalogue without waiting for Delia's response.

"Oh. Uh, sure," Delia mumbled. Well, she'd stuck herself with this one, hadn't she? But who would have imagined that Pamela intended to start inventory immediately?

Pamela would be an efficient head librarian, of that Delia was certain. But Pamela, handy at organizing what had previously been a rather haphazardly run library, didn't have any aptitude with people. Now, Estelle ... she could deal with patrons, from the toddler whose mother thought of the library as a convenient baby-sitting service to ninety-three-year-old Mrs. Whitlock, who sometimes used her partial as a bookmark and forgot to remove it before returning the book. Estelle's soft Southern drawl and well-bred manner had won her the undying devotion of almost everyone who'd ever set foot in the library. Delia sighed and told herself that eras passed all the time without anyone noticing. But certainly Estelle's death had hastened the end of the genteel South in Jesus Creek. If it had ever really existed.

Pamela had not only cleaned up the disorder left in the office, she'd also rearranged the remaining furniture and organized the bookcase that held books yet to be processed.

"You did all this today?" Delia asked, looking at her watch and noticing that it was barely eleven o'clock.

"I started at five," Pam told her. "I've already gone through the catalogue and put that in order. Now that you're here we can get started on the inventory. Here's what we'll do. You hold the cards and call them off. I'll check the shelves."

"Fine," Delia said. "But you do know that this isn't necessary. No one expects you to put in this kind of effort while you're obviously still in shock."

"It needs doing and it might as well be done now. Once we get this out of the way, the library will run more efficiently. Keeping track of it all will be that much easier for me." Pamela stood with her hands firmly on her hips, as if daring Delia to disagree.

"Yoo-hoo!" Frankie Mae's voice came from the back door.

"Good Lord, it's that woman again." Pamela sighed and rolled her eyes. "She expects undivided attention to her silly rattling."

Frankie Mae was dressed as she had been the night of the fire, except the pith helmet had been replaced by a straw gardening hat and a rolled-up newspaper was stuck in the back pocket of her

pants. "Saw your car parked out there," she said to
Pam. "Didn't think you'd be here today."

"There's a lot of work to complete before we reopen on Thursday," Pam told her bluntly.

"Can't open on Thursday," Frankie Mae said
firmly. "Estelle's funeral."

"We aren't open today, at any rate," Pamela said
stiffly.

"Well, as long as the door's open I figured I could
come on in. I only need one book."

"Do you think it's a good idea to leave the back
door open?" Delia asked.

Pamela ignored her. "I told you, Frankie, we
aren't open for business. We're attempting to do
inventory."

"How you gonna do that? You haven't called in
all the books. Can't do inventory without at least a
month's notice to the patrons."

"We'll deal with the books that are checked out
after we've finished with the ones on the shelves."

"Fine, then I won't be any problem to you. I just
want to look at one here in the library."

"Oh, for goodness' sake, Frankie Mae." Pamela
shook her head in disgust. "All right, what do you
want?"

"This new history of Jesus Creek," Frankie Mae
said. "The one in the *Headlight*." She pulled the
previous day's newspaper from her back pocket and
held it out for them to see.

Delia took the paper and scanned the front page.
City council couldn't agree on a budget, the Christmas parade had been scheduled, and—there it was—
a picture of Estelle and Oliver Host. The caption
read: "New book purchased by library. Oliver Host
recently published *The Complete History of Origi-*

nal Families of Jesus Creek, and a copy may now be found in the Jesus Creek Public Library. Head Librarian Estelle Carhart is seen here receiving a copy of the book from its author."

"I didn't know Oliver had finished this," Delia said. "He's been talking about it for years."

"Oh, that." Pamela said. "He finished it, all right. Had a few copies printed and now he calls himself an author. Do you know that the board approved the purchase of that book? Oliver charged us forty dollars!"

Delia was stunned. Forty dollars? Surely Pamela was exaggerating. No one in his right mind would buy—or even try to sell—such a book at that exorbitant price.

"Well, at any rate," said Frankie Mae, "I'd like to see this copy."

"I don't know if it's been processed," Pamela said. "He only gave it to us a few days ago."

"What difference does it make? I don't want to check it out. I just want to look at it."

"That won't hurt, will it, Pam?" Delia said. "She could read in the office while we're checking shelves."

"I suppose," Pamela said grudgingly. "Let's go find it."

Frankie Mae and Delia followed her into the office, where Frankie Mae settled into a chair and arranged her notebook on the desk in front of her. Pamela began to run her finger along the books lined neatly on the bookshelves. "This is time I can't afford to waste," she grumbled. "It will take every minute of the next three days to prepare for opening."

"I can hunt for the book if you want to get started on inventory," Delia offered.

"No. Neither of you should even be in here," Pamela told her firmly. "This is the office, for employee use only."

Frankie Mae snorted. "People been using this room for years, for everything from eating lunch to fooling around with the postman."

"I beg your pardon." Pamela stopped and turned to face Frankie Mae.

"Before your time," Frankie Mae said with a sly grin.

"Well, the book isn't here," Pamela said. "So you're out of luck anyway."

"Where is it, then? Don't tell me you've lost it."

"It must be out front. I guess Estelle processed it one day when I wasn't here."

"Then let's look for it there," Frankie Mae said, rising from her chair. "I want to have a gander at that book before everybody in the club gets in here to haggle over it."

"What's so special about it, anyway?" Pamela asked. "You and Estelle have surely dug up every bit of information on your family by now, haven't you?"

Estelle had completed her own family history long before she married Walter Carhart, whereupon she had started on *his* family pedigree. Walter's sister, Frankie Mae, had never approved of the marriage, since she considered Estelle "a popbrained idiot" and had consistently refused to share any of her research. For that reason, Estelle had been forced to start from scratch when she'd decided to document the Carharts.

"Edwin's," Frankie Mae said. Edwin was her late

husband, another descendant of the original settlers. "Thought I'd give a complete chart to the kids
for Christmas. Just possible Oliver found something new."

"Your kids couldn't care less about their roots,
Frankie Mae," Pamela snapped. "Honestly, I don't
know why anyone would give two hoots about a
bunch of dead relatives anyway."

"Figures," Frankie Mae snorted. "I wouldn't think
you'd have any ancestors you'd want to remember."

"Why don't we check the catalogue?" Delia suggested quickly. "It's certainly in the genealogy section. Then Frankie can get to work and so can we."

Pamela reluctantly began to dig through the catalogue while Frankie Mae stood behind her, looking over her shoulder. Delia, meanwhile, tucked her
coat, scarf, hat, and gloves into the office shelves.
There was nothing in the world that could make
her open that closet door and hang her belongings
there.

For twenty years Estelle Carhart had run the library in her charming but slipshod manner. It
wasn't unusual for Estelle to send someone out the
door without checking their books, especially if she
happened to be engaged in an interesting conversation at the time. Nor was it unusual for her to
excuse late books if the reader claimed to have intended to return them on time. To Estelle, good in-
tentions were as good as fact.

It was clear that things were about to change
drastically. While Pamela Satterfield had only been
with the library a short time, she had very definite,
very rigid ideas of how the place should be run.
Delia had often seen her scurrying around behind
Estelle, trying to catch those unchecked books be-

fore they got out the door or trying to collect late fines from people who'd already been excused by Estelle. Now that Pamela would be moving up to the position of head librarian, the patrons had better shape up.

"Not here," Pamela said. "Estelle probably just put it on the shelf without making a card for it. We'll have to go through the genealogy section."

"Why don't you let me do that?" Delia offered. "That's my specialty, anyway. You go ahead and start the inventory."

Pamela pursed her lips, which Delia interpreted as agreement. "Come on, Frankie Mae," Delia said. "There aren't that many books in this section. Shouldn't take too long."

Frankie Mae didn't wait until Pamela was out of sight to begin complaining. "Woman's a regular bitch. Don't know how she expects people to appreciate their library when she's always harping."

"Now, Frankie. Pamela had a terrible shock. You can't imagine how it was yesterday. On top of that she's had to take over every detail of running this place without a minute's notice. It's a lot of responsibility."

"Don't be naive, Delia. She's been trying to take over for years. It's been a blasted battleground around here, what with her trying to make Estelle look stupid. Not that it was all that hard to do."

"Frankie!"

"What? You think just because she's dead, people are gonna forget how dumb she was?"

"Probably not. But I don't see any need to dwell on it, do you?"

Frankie shook her head. "You plant somebody, and all of a sudden she's a saint."

Delia scanned the books in the genealogy corner, pointedly ignoring Frankie Mae's further comments. "Nothing here," she said. "I'd better look again. It must be here somewhere."

"Not necessarily," Frankie offered. "Pamela may be a pain in the tail but she's right about one thing. Estelle never could get anything done right. That book may be sitting under a flowerpot somewhere."

"Well, it's definitely not here. Look, we're bound to find it when we do the inventory. I'll make a note to call you as soon as we do and then you can come in and look at it, okay?"

"Guess that's the best I can hope for," Frankie said. "I'll just go on home and wait. Try to hurry up, though."

With Frankie Mae gone and Pamela roaming the shelves, Delia looked once more through the volumes listed under genealogy. The book was certainly not there. Possibly Estelle had put it under reference books, she thought. "I'm going to check for Oliver's book in reference," she told Pamela.

"Sounds like a reasonable place to shelve it."

"*Genealogy* is a reasonable place to shelve it," Pamela said.

"Well, yes. But if it's not there, the next most logical place is reference." Delia pulled a stepladder to the reference shelves and began checking titles. "I'm looking forward to reading it myself. After all these years of listening to Oliver talk about it, I'm glad it's done."

"Big deal," Pamela said. "He dug around the state archives for a few years and finally had to take the thing to a printer. No real publisher would touch it."

"Well, I don't suppose there'll be a great demand for it," Delia admitted. "Except in Jesus Creek."

"Not much demand here, either."

"I can tell you, all the members of the SDC and the Historical Society will eat it up. Of course, most of them will be looking for a misspelled name or inaccurate date."

"Let me know when you're through over there. We'll start inventory." Pamela could not have been less interested in what Delia was saying. She was a relative newcomer to Jesus Creek and had not been raised to savor bloodlines.

"Why don't we begin here? One place is as good as another, isn't it?"

Pamela sighed and picked a piece of lint from her sweater—another of her original creations, Delia noticed. This one was white with a black rose pattern knitted into it. She wondered how Pamela found time to make her own clothes when she worked at least ten hours a day. One assumed she had some sort of personal life, hobbies, friends, and family to occupy her. Then again, extremely efficient people always did find time for things.

Poor Estelle had never seemed to accomplish anything. Whenever Delia had visited her house, there'd always been a layer of dust on the fine old furniture, cat hair on anything that collected it, and a pile of dishes in the sink. Estelle had never seemed to be in touch with the rest of the planet. She spoke of her Confederate ancestors with pride, as if Great-Grandpa Halland had just last week come home from Stone's River with his wounds. Estelle's accent carried the soft r that had to be cultivated—and usually was—by the plantation set, as Delia thought of them. Her parents had the accent,

too, so it probably came naturally to Estelle. Those
old families fortunate enough to have retained their
fortunes throughout the Civil War and afterward
(and even the ones who had not) could at least pretend they'd maintained the purity of the Old South.

Eventually everything had come to Estelle. Now
the fortune would be passed on to Walt Jr., the last
of the line. With Walt Jr. grown and Walt Sr. dead
these last five years, Estelle had devoted her life to
preserving her little corner of the Confederacy.
She'd held afternoon teas on the lawn, playing
hostess to the few old ladies who could be counted
on to arrive in hats and gloves. Perhaps Estelle
wouldn't have minded her own death after all.
There was very little of her world left in which to
live.

"It doesn't seem to be here, either," Delia said,
climbing down from the stepladder. "Where else
might Estelle have kept it?"

"I wouldn't begin to guess," Pamela said. She'd
been checking off cards as she found the corre-
sponding book. "But if we get on with this inventory, maybe you'll find it."

"Oh, yes. Of course." Delia patted her hair into
place, feeling thoroughly chastised. Funny how
Pamela could make her feel like an unruly child.
Well, she supposed everyone had to have a talent
of some sort.

By the end of the day Delia felt as if she'd been
rolled in dust and popped into the oven to bake.
Most of the library books would have been checked
out often enough to have been wiped clean, but the
entire reference shelf seemed to have been untouched for decades, judging by the amount of grime

that had built up on them. Pamela had insisted on cleaning as well as inventory updating, and since Delia was the one on the ladder pulling down books and checking their numbers, she'd naturally been assigned the dust cloth.

If one of the Friends didn't agree to help out, Delia would have to return tomorrow and continue inventory with Pamela. No doubt Frankie Mae would be there, too, demanding that they find that book she'd wanted.

Since they hadn't yet unearthed Oliver's book, Delia decided to call the author himself and ask to borrow a copy. Or perhaps she'd buy one, she thought as she dialed Oliver's number. Her own collection of genealogical sources was small, since most information was contained in government records and couldn't be purchased, only copied. Besides, Oliver wasn't likely to sell many and she felt sorry for him. *The Original Families of Jesus Creek* would make a welcome addition to her personal library.

"The number you have reached has been disconnected," the nasal voice told her. "If you need assistance, please hang up and dial the information operator."

She'd dialed Oliver's home phone without thinking. But where on earth might the man be staying? Oliver was a difficult person to get along with. Delia couldn't imagine that anyone had invited him to move in. There was one person in town, other than Constance Winter, who would certainly know the movements of everyone else. She dialed Roger's number from memory.

Roger's answering machine picked up on the third ring. "Not here," it said. "Or here but don't wish to speak to anyone. Either way, leave your name and number and I'll think about calling you back."

"Roger," Delia said loudly. "Pick up the phone. Right now."

There was a brief silence, a click, and Roger's voice. "Good evening, Delia," he said haughtily. "Why don't you leave a message like any normal person would and assume that I'll get back to you?"

"I don't like those stupid things, Roger. Besides, why should I talk to a machine when I know perfectly well that you're sitting there listening anyway?"

"My, my," Roger said. "We've had a bad day, haven't we? Shall I pop over there and give you a back rub?"

"Always appreciated, dear. But first a question. Do you have any idea where Oliver Host might be living?"

"Oliver? What on earth do you want with Oliver?"

"There's supposed to be a copy of the book he wrote in the library, but we can't find it. I thought I'd buy a copy for my own use."

"Ah-ha. Well. It seems to me that I heard something about his moving into the inn for a while." Roger was eating. Delia could tell from the way he garbled every other word.

"Serves him right," Delia said, thinking of the quality of food and service at Twin Elms Inn, now that Patrick McCullough was running the place without his sister's help. Kate McCullough Yancy had been a whirlwind of efficiency, but she'd recently moved to west Tennessee, leaving Patrick to struggle with management of the inn, as well as juggling his insurance business and his duties as mayor of Jesus Creek. "If Oliver didn't constantly alienate people, maybe he'd have a friend who could put him up."

"Speaking of friends, I'm awfully cold over here tonight. Eating soup from the can, shivering in the corner of my poorly insulated room . . ."

"Are you hoping for an invitation?" Delia asked. Of course he was. He'd spent half the previous evening telling her how much he'd missed her during their respective holiday visits with their families. Delia had reminded him that she had been away only two days, while he'd returned home late Sunday night after a week's absence.

"How sweet. I'd love to join you for dinner. And after." Roger hung up quickly. It would take him approximately five minutes to get to her house, assuming his car started and he didn't drive it into a ditch on the way.

Delia was on the front porch with Reb Gassler when Roger arrived. Since Reb had parked the patrol car in the driveway beside Delia's sensible Ford, Roger was forced to park on the street. Delia knew he'd grumble, since he considered curbside parking not only inconvenient, but dangerous as well.

"Hello, Shelton." Reb nodded briskly.

"Is she under arrest?" Roger asked, slipping one arm around Delia's waist to stake his territory.

"Don't be ridiculous, Roger," Delia told him. "I'm a law-abiding citizen. And even if I chose a life of crime, Reb couldn't arrest me. I know too much about him."

"I'm looking into Estelle's death," Reb explained. "Delia was unlucky enough to find the body, so she gets questioned more than anybody else."

"Remember that, Delia," Roger said. "Next time you find a corpse, don't report it."

Delia didn't laugh. "I was just telling Reb that even if I'd seen anything out of the ordinary, I certainly wouldn't have paid attention to it after finding Estelle. Quite frankly, I don't even remember calling him. I don't remember anything except the way she looked."

Reb nodded sympathetically. "I know. And I hate like hell to have to bother you again. But we're stuck. Any fingerprints that might have been there are lost in the jumble. Too damned many people wandering in and out of that place, you know?"

"Pamela will put a quick end to that," Delia assured him.

"Has Estelle ever gone into the library in the middle of the night before?"

Delia shook her head. "I wouldn't think so. That sounds like something Pam would do, though. She's a workaholic."

Reb looked up sharply. "You reckon anybody'd have expected to find *her* there, then?"

"I don't think anyone would have expected to find her, no. Why would anyone be in the library after closing? Reb, it has to be something the intruder wanted. Books, money, or maybe even something less likely than that. A typewriter, maybe?"

Reb made a quick note on his pad. "What else is in the library?" he asked, without looking up. "I don't know much about the place. Is there anything at all that some nut might want?"

Delia thought about it carefully for a moment. There were the new chairs Pamela had complained about, along with eating utensils used by the staff and possibly a few personal items that were left in the lost and found. Other than that, she couldn't think of a thing and told him so.

"You know," Reb said slowly, "at first I was sure it was just a kid, somebody who'd gone in there to tear up the place. But a kid wouldn't have killed her, you know? He'd have just run, wouldn't he?"

"But what else could it be, Reb?" Delia demanded. "No one would have hurt Estelle."

"Oh, I don't know," Roger put in. "I know there've been many times when the thought has crossed my mind."

"Hush, dear," Delia warned. "Reb will arrest you on suspicion."

"I'll sure keep him in mind," Reb said. He pocketed his notepad and pencil before stepping down off the porch. "If you come up with any ideas, give me a call. And kinda watch yourself, too. Whoever it was might think, since you found the body, you know more than you're telling." He crossed the yard to his car.

"Reb's tearing himself up about this," Delia pointed out.

"Really? How can you tell?"

"I know him. And to tell you the truth, Roger, so am I. I feel like I ought to have noticed more."

Roger gave her a reassuring squeeze. "That's ridiculous. If the police can't even find a fingerprint, what could there have been to notice?"

Delia sighed. Roger was right, of course. Still,

there had to be an explanation. She didn't believe in clueless crimes. As Reb had suggested, maybe she had noticed something. She'd just have to think about it some more.

CHAPTER

5

ELIZA WILSON LEACH WAS AN INTIMIDAT-
ing woman. Even Delia, who had known her since
childhood, tried to stay out of her way as much as
possible. Eliza was a tall, thin woman who, as a
child, had been all sharp angles and awkwardness.
Even in adulthood her bones were still obvious,
poking out here and there when she moved. It was
her family, and her husband's family, that gave her
power and the confidence to use it. She was also
head of the library board of directors and therefore
the appropriate person to help with the current crisis.

The Leach home was a gracious antebellum
structure, surrounded now by dozens of frame and
brick dwellings that had been built during different
periods and in vastly different styles. The acres that
had originally been part of the Leach estate were
sold off in pieces over the years until, by the time
Eliza married into the family, there was nothing
left except the half-acre lot on which the house

stood. Eliza hated the houses that stood around hers and despised the circumstances that had forced various Leaches to allow those homes to be built there. Since there was nothing she could do about it now (aside from her frequent attempts to buy out the neighbors so that she could have their homes demolished), she'd chosen to put up blinders. Literally.

Either side of her property was bordered with hedge and trellises covered with thick, flowering vines. Since the Leach house sat back away from the one-way street it fronted, there was plenty of room for weeping willows to shade the yard and shield Eliza from the passing traffic. Delia thought it was working out well for Eliza. If nothing else, the neighbors wouldn't bother her because the meticulously landscaped front yard was so intimidating, just like the woman who'd arranged it.

Delia turned onto the cobbled walkway from the sidewalk. "Eliza!" she called as she recognized the figure dressed in gray slacks and a heavy gray sweater. "Isn't it too cold for gardening?"

Eliza looked up and waved with her towel. She was on her knees, digging around in the azalea bed beside the wide front porch. "This weather can't last much longer," Eliza said. "I might as well get the mulching done and save the good days for something else."

There were those in Jesus Creek who believed that Eliza Wilson Leach loved nature. For proof, they pointed to her habit of rising before dawn in spring and summer to put a full day's work into her flower gardens and vegetable patch. But Delia suspected that it was not *love* for nature that motivated Eliza. Rather, it seemed as if she wanted to *conquer* it. Nothing was allowed to grow wild or misshapen. Roses had been planted according to a color plan, and the vegetables seemed less important to Eliza than the size and shape of the garden and the straightness of the rows.

As Delia neared the porch, Eliza's only child, Lindsay James, came out the front door, carrying a heavy coat over his arm. The new owner and publisher of the *Jesus Creek Headlight* wore the pleading expression of a five-year-old, offering his mother a handful of flowers picked from her rose garden. "Mother, I think you should put this on," he said, before noticing Delia.

"I'm just fine, Lindsay James," Eliza said brusquely. "If I'd needed a coat, I'd have worn one. Well, aren't you going to speak to Delia?"

"Sorry." Lindsay James stood there like a mannequin, no longer certain what to do with the coat. It seemed no time had passed since he'd been a little boy in Delia's class, always struggling for perfect grades to please his mother. "How are you, Delia? I heard you had a nasty shock the other day."

"I'm fine, Lindsay James. But I've just come from the library, and frankly, I think Pamela is a mess."

Eliza sat back on her heels and looked up at Delia, squinting against the wind that whipped around the corner of the porch. "Why?" she asked. "What's the matter with her?"

"She's hyper, for one thing," Delia said. "Wound up like a top. She's over there just going to town on inventory. Even roped me into it, as a matter-of-fact."

"I'm sorry to hear she's taken Estelle's death so

badly, but I don't know what any of us can do about it," Eliza said matter-of-factly.

"One thing that would help is *help*. Some of the usual volunteers are nervous about going back to work. Understandably, I guess. But the place was understaffed to start with, Eliza, you know that."

Eliza sighed. "Yes, but there's only so much money to go around. We have to make do with what's available."

"I realize that. The problem is that money or no money, you're going to have to hire a new assistant librarian. Either that or convince the Friends to put aside their squeamishness and show up."

Eliza put her trowel carefully into her gardening basket. "How many regular volunteers are there?" she asked.

"Twenty, give or take. But I've spoken to all of them, and there's not a single one who can work full-time until next week at the earliest."

Eliza considered for a moment. "What about you?"

"I was afraid you'd ask that. The truth is, Eliza, I'd be very little help. I've been chipping in this morning, but my specialty is genealogy. Pamela would have to waste half her days telling me what to do and how to do it. We need someone with real hands-on library experience."

Eliza pursed her skinny lips and made clicking noises, either as proof that she was puzzling over a solution or as an indication that she was irritated by the whole discussion.

Lindsay leaned slightly forward and said timidly, "I may have an idea."

Delia and Eliza both turned to him. It wasn't often that Lindsay expressed an opinion in his mother's presence, and both women were mildly shocked that he was doing so now.

"Perhaps Sarah Elizabeth could do it," he said.

Sarah Elizabeth was Eliza's daughter-in-law of two months. Delia had met the girl briefly at the wedding reception. She seemed pleasant enough, but it's hard to tell about a bride on her wedding day; therefore, Delia had postponed her permanent opinion. "Does she know anything about libraries?" she asked cautiously.

Eliza almost smiled. "Why, certainly. She had planned to take a degree in library science, in fact, before she married Lindsay James."

"Well," Delia said, endeavoring to think of a reason why this plan wouldn't be feasible. Aside from the obvious one, of course: Sarah Elizabeth was barely more than a teenager and, at the reception, had seemed even more nervous than Lindsay James. Delia suspected Pamela would eat her alive.

"We'll discuss it with her right away," Eliza said. "She should be around here somewhere. Lindsay James, go get her. You can talk to her yourself, Delia, and see how qualified she is."

Lindsay James sighed and went inside to search for his wife. He was a nice enough man, Delia imagined—up to a point. He was tall and thin like his mother, with his father's looks and disquieting habit of catering to Eliza's every whim. Delia was somehow put off by the way he'd characteristically refused to assert himself in his mother's presence. Oh, well. She was probably being unfair to the man. No one could doubt that he was a good and devoted son, and those were certainly in short supply lately.

Delia wondered if Sarah Elizabeth had been chosen to marry Lindsay James simply because of her

name. It was tradition in the Leach family to call
members by both first and middle names and, on a
few rare occasions, by all three names. This was
done primarily to distinguish between Sarah Elizabeth Conway Leach and her mother, Sarah Elizabeth
Conway. There had, at one time or another, been a
Lindsay James Leach along with Lindsay Young
Leach. When only one person with a particular
name remained alive, it was acceptable to drop the
middle name. Consequently, after Eliza's mother,
Eliza Claire, died, Eliza had instantly ceased to be
Eliza Marion.

Delia suspected that the tradition held because
all those names sounded quite formal. If ever a family adhered to formality, it was the Leaches.

"Here's Sarah Elizabeth," Lindsay James said,
returning with his wife and making the simple
statement sound like a royal introduction.

Sarah Elizabeth was as tall as Eliza but softer
around the edges. She had a perfectly smooth face,
naturally, which made her appear less than completely formed. But in her simple, youthful slacks
and sweater, she appeared fresh and alive. Quite a
contrast to the monochromatic surroundings.

"Hello, Delia," she said, grinning widely.

"Sarah Elizabeth. How nice to see you again."
Delia rose and held out her hand, suddenly feeling
as if she'd stepped into the queen's parlor. "I'm surprised you remember me. We've only met once,
haven't we?"

"I've seen you glued to the microfilm screen at
the library. Mother Eliza says you're into family
research. I've never done any of that myself, but I'd
like to someday. As far as I know, no one's ever dug

up any of my roots." Sarah Elizabeth gave a breathy little laugh at her own joke.

Delia couldn't help but warm to her, especially after she saw the look Eliza gave her daughter-in-law. "Why don't you give me a call sometime and I'll help you get started?" she offered. "If you have a family Bible, any kind of family records, get them together. It's really not difficult at all."

"That's so nice of you," Sarah Elizabeth said, wide-eyed. "Thank you, Delia."

"Sarah Elizabeth, you know perfectly well that I've been trying to help you develop an interest in family history," Eliza said sharply. It was just like her to ignore the fact that Sarah Elizabeth had merely been making polite conversation. "But that isn't what brought Delia here. We have something to tell you."

Sarah Elizabeth waited patiently, seemingly oblivious of Eliza's reprimand. Apparently she was already accustomed to her mother-in-law's high-handed attitude.

"Now then." Eliza stood up and brushed at her slacks. "Since Estelle's death, the library has been shorthanded. Unfortunately there's not one among the Friends of the Library who can fill in. I've suggested to Delia and Lindsay James that you could make yourself useful."

"We just need someone until the board hires a permanent replacement," Delia explained rather more tactfully. "Pamela is swamped with work and there's absolutely no way she can handle everything."

Sarah Elizabeth frowned. "Temporary. Oh, well. I suppose it's for a good cause." She turned to look at Lindsay James. "What do you think, honey?"

Lindsay James glanced at his mother, who nodded firmly. "I think it's a great idea," he said enthusiastically.

"Well then." Sarah Elizabeth took a deep breath and smiled. "I guess I'll do it. When will I start?"

"How about immediately?" Delia asked. "And thank you so much, Sarah Elizabeth. I had no idea until Eliza mentioned it that you'd majored in library science."

"Only one year. I met Lindsay James during freshman orientation." Sarah Elizabeth glanced shyly at her husband, who seemed not to notice.

"Oh. I'm sure Pamela can explain all the procedures. The library will be closed tomorrow for Estelle's funeral, but you'll be there first thing Friday, right?"

"Start going through your closets," Eliza said. "You'll need a professional wardrobe. I'll come up to help in a bit. Lindsay James, go along and help her pick out a few things for next week."

Lindsay James mumbled a few words to Delia and followed his wife into the house. He still had the coat draped over his arm.

"What a lovely girl!" Delia said. "You must be delighted to have her in the family."

Eliza made no comment. Delia should have known that Eliza, of all people, wouldn't approve of any match her only child had made. She'd probably been hoping for European aristocracy at the very least.

"Thank you for tending to that, Eliza. Do you know how soon the board will hire a replacement?"

"Possibly in a few weeks or a month. Don't worry about it, Delia. I'm sure the board will act with the greatest speed."

"Yes. I'm sure. Well, it's been lovely chatting with you, Eliza. We should get together more often." Even though she and Eliza had been lifelong acquaintances, Delia had never been really comfortable around the woman. "I guess after what happened to Estelle I'm feeling melancholy, but I suddenly want to keep all my old friends around me. We lose touch, don't we? And forget about each other altogether sometimes. Then something like this happens, and it seems . . . I don't know. As if we're losing each other so quickly."

For a moment Eliza's stern exterior disappeared and she wore the wistful expression that Delia remembered from years before. "I know exactly what you mean." Eliza even smiled a little. "Hard to believe it's been over twenty-five years since high school. If you'll recall, I tried to suggest that we all attend the same college. That might have helped keep us together."

Eliza had, indeed, made that suggestion. Margaret, Estelle, and Eliza—for a while there it had been iffy and Delia had worried that she would never get away from the other three. Not that she didn't love them dearly, but college had been her chance (as she'd seen it then) to break restrictive ties and explore the world. At the last minute, thankfully, Margaret had met that air-force fellow and then Estelle had broken her courtship with Franklin James Leach—which had prompted her to choose *any* college he was not attending. By that time Eliza had abandoned the whole idea of continued sisterhood, partially, Delia suspected, because she'd snatched Franklin James up as quickly as Estelle had dropped him. After that, Eliza had little time for her old girlfriends.

"Remember how our parents used to tell us that time moved faster as you got older? We were always complaining about being too young to do what we wanted, always so eager to grow up."

"Perfectly normal for children to want that. And equally normal for us to wallow in the past."

"Speaking of wallowing, I'm meeting Oliver Host for lunch. I hate to think of that beautiful old house being gone. It was a Jesus Creek landmark even before I was born."

"Even before your mother was born. But why on earth are you meeting Oliver? I seem to recall that you never could stand the man." Eliza seemed genuinely startled.

"That book he wrote—the one he's been carrying on about all these years. He placed a copy in the library. But we haven't been able to find it. Of course, Pamela isn't finished with inventory yet. I'm sure Estelle just put the book in some unlikely place. In the meantime I was hoping to get another copy from Oliver."

"Well, Delia, really. Why would you want to read a book by that old bore? Haven't you heard him rattle on endlessly about Jesus Creek history? It's mostly *his* history, actually. The only facts he's ever bothered to verify inevitably recount the heroic deeds of his ancestors."

"I thought I'd buy a copy for myself. It could be that he's discovered some piece of information that I don't have in my records. But mostly I want it because it's a book by a hometown author. Maybe I'll get him to autograph it. You shouldn't be so hard on him, Eliza. After all, it's not as if Oliver has any heroic deeds of his own to brag about."

"Uhm." Eliza almost laughed that time. "Well,

good luck then. I hope Oliver doesn't back you into a corner and talk your ear off."

"I'll be prepared for a quick getaway. The only people who get trapped by Oliver more than once are masochists."

"See you Monday night, then," Eliza said. "SDC meeting. I hear that a history professor from Austin Peay will be explaining the effectiveness of Confederate strategy at First Manassas."

"Oh, thrilling," said Delia, who had never been keen about battles of The War. "Well, we can always hope that Oliver will debate the guest and wind up giving us his version of the campaign. With luck, a full-fledged brawl could break out."

Oliver was waiting for her at Eloise's Diner on the courthouse square. He'd chosen a booth in back and had already ordered his own lunch. By the time Delia arrived he was boring the other customers with a detailed account of the fire. Oliver was an attractive man until you got to know him. His physique and profile were pure Hollywood, and when he wanted to be, he was charming. As a child he'd taken pleasure in sneaking up behind his playmates (one of whom had been Delia) and grabbing the back of their necks in a pinch hold. The only improvement, as far as Delia could see, was that adulthood had given him better taste in clothes.

"Good afternoon, Oliver," Delia said, sliding into the booth and facing him. "I'm so sorry to hear about your house. But thank goodness you weren't hurt."

"Oh, but I was. I'd think you, of all people, would understand how much my loss means." Oliver shook his head mournfully.

"I beg your pardon?"

"All my research. Irreplaceable documents. Vast collections of photographs, Linotypes. All gone in a blaze of evil-inspired arson."

Oliver was still shaking his head and now began to wring his hands as well. Delia would have suspected that he was on the verge of tears if she hadn't known him better. That gleam in his eye meant trouble for someone, although at this point she couldn't imagine for whom.

"I certainly sympathize. I'd hate to lose my little bit of family research—and mine is nothing compared to yours."

Oliver nodded agreement. "And not only my family research, but the history, the lives of almost every original resident of Jesus Creek."

Eloise approached cautiously to take Delia's order, casting a few wary glances at Oliver. Delia recognized the symptoms. The woman had probably been forced to listen to an account of Oliver's work before he'd placed his order.

"A vegetable plate and coffee," Delia said quickly, releasing Eloise before Oliver had time to notice her.

"The work of a lifetime," Oliver went on, "wiped out in a single night. I don't doubt for a minute that it was done by some of my rivals."

"Rivals?" Delia asked, then realized that she probably didn't want to hear the explanation. "Reb mentioned arson," she said quickly.

"Oh, yes." Oliver sawed at his pork chop as he spoke. "The fire chief had no trouble finding the cause of the blaze. Why, the empty gas can was left right beside the house."

"Really? Not very clever."

"No. I've always said, if one intends to commit criminal acts, one should pursue that career meticulously. This sort of sloppy performance cannot be excused."

Delia was amazed at Oliver's dichotomous evaluation of the event. What other burned-out homeowner would analyze the shoddy way a fire had been started? "What are you going to do now, Oliver?"

"Why, begin again. What else is there? I plan to rebuild the house exactly as it was. It will be impossible to get the same quality of materials, of course. Still, I'll rise to the occasion. As you well know, Delia, I am not a quitter." He poked his fork at her to emphasize this.

"Good for you," Delia said. "That's a great attitude."

"Of course, I'm dreadfully upset about the library."

Delia nodded. "That was horrible," she agreed.

"Dreadful. Just dreadful. How anyone could be so cruel is beyond my comprehension."

"I suppose you've heard the funeral will be to-morrow."

"Funeral?" Oliver seemed to be completely baffled.

"Estelle's funeral."

"Estelle? Oh, that's right. She's dead, isn't she?"

Now Delia was confused. "Haven't we just been talking about that?"

"Not to my knowledge. You may have been talking about most anything. I have been talking about the damage done to my library and the precious documents therein."

"Oh. I see." Delia was struck for a moment by

what appeared to be Oliver's lack of compassion. Of
course, he'd suffered a tremendous loss himself and
perhaps he just wasn't rational.

"The fire started there. Everything incinerated
in a matter of minutes. It pains me to imagine how
quickly those brittle, yellowed papers must have
been consumed. The only traces of people who once
lived and created life—"

"Oliver, please. Let me get a word in here. I'm interested in your book. I understand there's a copy in
the library. The public library, that is. Unfortunately, what with Estelle's death and all, we haven't
been able to locate it."

"That madwoman has probably called it into service as a child's booster seat. No respect for history,
that Estelle. Always ignored the facts and put forth
some silly, romanticized version of the past."

"At any rate," Delia went on, "may I get a copy
from you? I'd like to buy one—autographed, of
course."

"Haven't you heard a word I've said to you,
Delia? My library is gone. Gone! All the copies of
Jesus Creek Families were destroyed in the confla-
gration."

"Oh!" Delia should have realized that would be
the case. For some reason, though, she'd envisioned
Oliver carrying around a few dozen copies of his
book at all times. "Well, that is terrible. But won't
the printer be able to run off some more?"

"Of course my ... *publisher* will, Delia. But not
right away. It could be two or three months before
he gets to it. I've already spoken with him and tried
to urge him to greater speed but—"

"So the only copy of your book is the one in the
library?"

"Correct," Oliver said. "And the one I have."

"Oh, you do have one then?"

"Technically it's not mine. You see, I meant to give it to Eliza Leach, since her family played such a great role in the settling of Jesus Creek. But I completely forgot, what with all that's been happening to me lately."

"The copy for Eliza wasn't in your library?"

"Why, no. I'd taken it with me when I went to dinner."

So he *did* carry his books with him. "Where did you have dinner?"

"At the Leach home, of course. They'd invited me for dinner and I'd intended the book as an after-dinner treat. Unfortunately I became so bored by the conversation that I forgot to mention it to her. I discovered it on the seat of my car a day or so later. Otherwise I'd have nothing at all to show for my effort."

"That's fortunate. At least you still have a copy for yourself. And in time the printer will give you more." Delia was not about to fall in with his pretense that he had a bona fide publisher. Oliver had taken the manuscript down to the newspaper and print shop and paid to have it done, as every one in town knew full well.

"Exactly. And I plan to get things rolling this very afternoon." Oliver leaned back in his chair and hooked his thumbs into the lapels of his suit jacket. "Do I understand that you want to order a copy?"

"What? Oh, yes. That would be lovely, Oliver. And in the meantime do you suppose I might borrow your copy?"

Oliver shook his head vigorously. "No, no, my dear Delia. I couldn't possibly. Too risky. No, you'll just have to wait for the next printing like everyone else."

Delia sighed. She'd known Oliver all his life, and there was no question that the book would be an arcane accumulation arranged in some convoluted pattern that only Oliver could comprehend. Maybe she didn't want to read it, after all.

"And speaking of my evening with Eliza, I have to tell you"—Oliver waved at Eloise for a coffee refill—"that to this day Eliza Leach hasn't gotten over Estelle and Franklin James."

Delia stared at him. Eliza's husband, Franklin James, had been dead for over two years. Surely if there'd been anything between him and Estelle, Delia would have heard about it by now.

"You know," Oliver went on after Eloise replenished his coffee, "I always suspected that Estelle and Franklin were simply having a spat."

"Excuse me, Oliver," Delia interrupted. "I haven't a clue here. What sort of spat would they have had?"

"You remember. Just before the end of our senior year, when everyone was making plans for the prom? Estelle and Franklin broke up—"

"But Oliver, that was over twenty-five years ago. What on earth has it got to do with Eliza today?"

"I'm trying to explain, Delia, if you'll kindly shut up and listen. Now then. If you'll recall, Estelle and Franklin had a lovers' quarrel, one of those teenage things. None of us believed the breakup would last. And most likely they'd have been prom dates had it not been for Eliza."

"Right. Eliza attended the prom with Franklin. And I spent most of the evening in the ladies' room with Estelle." Delia had missed most of the festivities while she'd patiently supplied tissues to a weepy Estelle. Apparently brokenhearted, Estelle had taken one look at Eliza and Franklin dancing together and had retreated to the powder room, leaving her own date to linger at the punch bowl.

"And after the prom, very shortly after, Eliza and Franklin were unofficially engaged. I don't remember now, but I suspect that Eliza sowed that story. Old Franklin never had a chance."

"So why do you think Eliza would be upset about his earlier relationship with Estelle? After all, he married Eliza."

Oliver nodded firmly. "That's it. Eliza, no matter how you look at it, was second string. Could anyone ever forget that?"

Delia would cheerfully have admitted that *she'd* certainly forgotten—in fact, the interpretation had never entered her mind—but Oliver didn't give her time to speak.

"The other night at dinner, when Estelle's name came up, I swear I saw the gleam of hatred in Eliza's eyes. No, I don't think she ever felt safe about Franklin. About his devotion, his loyalty to her. And that makes me wonder: do you suppose she had good reason to worry?"

"What? You think Estelle and Franklin were . . . that's silly. Estelle was positively batty about Walt. Did you ever see them together when she wasn't cooing like a lovebird?"

"Public appearance is not necessarily the same as private reality." Oliver sipped his coffee with satisfaction.

Delia knew Oliver. She knew that he was happiest when he was stirring up stories. She also knew that he wasn't above initiating this sort of rumor. The question was, did he have any evidence or was he creating from smoke and air? "Okay, Oliver, did you ever see or hear anything to indicate that Estelle was involved with Franklin? And let's remember, Franklin has been dead for years now. You'd need an excellent memory to recall anything from that long ago."

"I *have* an excellent memory," he assured her.

Delia threw her hands into the air. Oliver was far better at this game than she. No matter what facts she presented, he'd counter with some innuendo that absolutely no one could confirm or deny.

"Some things never change," Oliver said, calmly buttering a roll. "Not even after twenty-five years." He gave her his flashiest smile. "Say, aren't you going to eat anything?"

Delia took the bread from the oven while Roger chopped vegetables for a salad. "He's such a pompous old poop," she said. "The only book he's ever read, other than history of course, is *Taking Care of Number One.*"

"Oliver Host? He gives new meaning to pomposity. Surely you noticed before now."

"Oh, I've known it for some time. Maybe I was just in a particularly bad mood today."

Roger arranged sliced carrots in the bowl, then went to the spice jars for what he liked to call his secret to successful salads. It was Delia's opinion that the secret was her fresh, organically grown herbs, but she kept this to herself. "You're just teed off because he won't lend you his book. It probably doesn't contain any earth-shattering news. Actually, if I were boning up on genealogy and wanted to dig dirt on my illustrious ancestors, I'd call you. You know just about everything on the subject."

Delia smiled. "I suppose your next line is that I lived through the entire history of Jesus Creek."

"Well, I wasn't actually going to say it aloud." Roger seated himself at the small kitchen table and began to butter a slice of the hot bread. "So the fire was started deliberately. But by whom? Actually, come to think of it, half the town would probably delight in seeing Oliver's source of useless information go up in flames."

Delia tossed the salad, then served it up. "I wondered about that myself. Oliver is overbearing, true. But no one actually hates him. I don't think. It's more . . . well, I suspect that no one understands him."

"I understand him perfectly. The man doesn't have a life of his own, so he's moved permanently to the nineteenth century."

"Thin ice, Rog. I happen to be quite fond of that century myself."

"I hope you aren't planning to wear hoop skirts and prattle incessantly about the Late Unpleasantness."

"Of course not. I'd never get those skirts through my front door. They jus' don't make houses foah graceful women anymoah." She speared a piece of lettuce.

"Not the accent," Roger cried. "Preserve me. I think that whole war was fought for the purpose of eradicating dropped *ing*'s and dim *r*'s."

"You have no romance in your soul, Roger. Picture this. Spring. The magnolias are in bloom. The smell of honeysuckle wafts on the air. On the wide front lawn, just outside the plantation—"

"What's the name of the plantation?"

"Make one up. I can't create this whole fantasy for

you. Anyway, on the lawn genteel young ladies promenade with pastel parasols. Their gently swaying hoop skirts accentuate the tiny waists of the—"

"Not to mention their tiny brains."

"Oh, forget it. I should have known better than to take up with a Yankee in the first place." It wasn't exactly true. Roger was a Tennessean, too. He just had the misfortune to descend from a family of east Tennesseans, a family with obvious and proud ties to the Union.

Roger smiled tolerantly at her. "You know, sometimes I worry that you'll become like these other people. Like Eliza, for instance. She truly believes that the South is just days away from winning that war."

"We all believe that, Roger," Delia said sweetly.

"Seriously, Dee. Haven't you ever noticed the way Eliza rhapsodizes about her ancestors? Do you know that she keeps a portrait of Robert E. Lee hanging in the den?"

"Well, yes, now that you mention it. But you have to remember, Eliza's family was the one with the plantation. The rest of us are descended from plain old dirt farmers and laborers. The Leaches and Wilsons were quite prominent before the war."

"Lots of people were. But that's been well over a hundred years ago. Don't you agree it's time to get on with life?"

"Roger, there's this phenomenon about being Southern. You see, we're all still in mourning for the gentility we lost."

"*You* didn't lose it, Delia. You live exactly the way you've always lived. And besides, the antebellum South was never picture perfect. Thousands of

slaves were delighted to witness an end to the fine
Old South."

"Oh, I know, Roger. I'm not nuts, nor am I insensitive. But it's one of those cultural anomalies. Good
taken with bad, most people like to believe they
came from the greatest culture on earth. We have
even more reason to revere our past. It was pretty
much confiscated before we'd gotten through with
it. We never had the chance to outgrow it."

"It occurs to me that you never will outgrow it if
you don't stop trying to relive it."

"Eat your dinner, Roger," Delia said. "Afterward
I'll explain why we still hang Yankees from time
to time."

CHAPTER

6

ESTELLE'S FUNERAL WAS HELD ON THURS-
day morning in the church she'd attended for most
of her adult life. The pink coffin stood at the front,
covered by a massive pall of pink roses. Behind the
pulpit, Brother Wagoner waited patiently for the
mourners to settle comfortably into the pews while
the organist struggled with "Amazing Grace."

"*Southern* Baptist?" Roger said, then put his
hand to his mouth and faked a cough. "I've never
heard of Northern Baptist or—"

"Give it a rest," Delia whispered. "This is a funeral, for God's sake."

Roger sat up straighter and assumed a solemn
expression. He tried to focus on the roses draped
across the coffin, but that only made it more difficult for him to comport himself. "It would have
seemed more appropriate," Roger whispered, "to
have used magnolias. Slightly wilted ones." He had
to stifle another chuckle. Delia elbowed him, force-
fully but discreetly.

The elderly woman at the organ had shifted into "Just As I Am, Lord," and more elderly women near the front were sniffing into dainty lace handkerchiefs. Frankie Mae, in her all-purpose cotton dress and cardigan, held a Kleenex in her hand but didn't seem to be using it. Of course, Frankie Mae didn't hold with public displays of emotion. The entire Leach family occupied one of the front pews. Eliza, in stiff black dress and veiled hat, was staring straight ahead. You could always count on Eliza: she knew how to be dignified when the occasion demanded it. Lindsay James and Sarah Elizabeth each held a hymnal and appeared to be studying the words to the song that no one was singing.

In a rare gesture of generosity, Eliza had invited Pamela to sit with the Leaches in what was known as the Founder's Pew. Jesus Creek Southern Baptist Church had been built on land donated by a Leach forefather and in return latter-day Leaches had been assured permanent front-row rights. It was an honor, no doubt, but Delia thought rather a burdensome one. If you have your own pew, she reasoned, you have to show up for church whether you want to or not.

Brother Wagoner, the far-too-young-to-be-taken-seriously minister, began to arrange note cards. Delia liked the man, although she'd had little chance to get to know him, since she wasn't a member of his church. But she was also aware that most of the congregation found him not quite to their taste. She'd heard rumors that he'd been observed jogging in sweats and even playing touch football with some young people. This was not behavior the congregation expected from their preacher. In fact, if he were not a distant relative of Eliza's, he'd never have been hired for the job.

Raising his arms high above his head, young Brother Wagoner began. "Brothers and sisters . . ." The organist stopped playing and the assembled mourners stopped coughing and fidgeting.

"Brothers and sisters," Brother Wagoner repeated, "on this solemn occasion I am reminded of"—he peeked quickly at his notes—"One Corinthians, verse fifty-two, which reminds us that, 'In a moment, in the twinkling of an eye at the last trump the trumpet shall sound and the dead shall be raised incorruptible, and we shall be changed.'

"Estelle Carhart was a God-fearing woman, a woman who devoted her life to helping others, to sharing knowledge and making the world a little better for all of us. Brothers and sisters, I have no doubt that when that trumpet sounds, Estelle will be raised to greet the glorious face of God."

Delia began to glance around the room, curious about the reactions of those who had gathered to bid a final goodbye to Estelle. She'd learned long ago the only way she could avoid uncontrolled hysteria at funerals was to pretend there was nothing going on. If she studied the people around her as if they were all specimens, she'd be okay. Probably.

The Leaches in the front row were perfectly still, each one apparently engrossed in the eulogy. Sarah Elizabeth was wearing a simple black dress today, her hair swept back from her face and caught in a clasp at the back of her neck. Her ensemble should have looked elegant, but it somehow resembled one of those period costumes in novelty photo shops. Sitting between Lindsay James and Eliza, Sarah

Elizabeth looked even younger than usual, and thinner, as if she'd been squeezed to fit.

Pamela kept a handkerchief pressed to her face most of the time. Delia thought that the poor woman must have only now realized the enormity of what had happened. Not an uncommon reaction. In the first few days after a death, there was so much activity. Pamela had kept busy with the library chores. Now, with nothing left to do, nothing to occupy her mind, Pamela might be on the verge of a breakdown. Delia hoped it wouldn't happen until after the service.

Since Delia had carefully avoided the funeral home, she'd not realized until the present moment that Walt Jr. was in from Nashville. He sat in the left front pew alone, listening attentively to Brother Wagoner. Delia realized she'd expected Estelle's friends to gather around him now, to offer support and comfort, but that was not the case. Apparently they felt that by moving away, Walt had somehow betrayed the legacy, and they were not prepared to accept him back into the fold.

Walt Jr. had always been a handsome boy, having inherited the best of both his parents. And so far as Delia knew, he'd adored his mother and never given her a minute of grief. According to Estelle, Walt had a job in the medical sciences (Estelle had never been quite clear about what it was he did). She'd often mentioned that she expected him to return to Jesus Creek to settle into the family home once he'd married some nice young girl. Delia wondered if he'd do that now—move home, that was— or if he'd sell the place.

"Change is an inevitable part of all our lives,"

Brother Wagoner was saying. "Death, too, has a place in Our Heavenly Father's plan."

Oliver Host had shown up for the funeral as well. Delia wasn't sure why that surprised her. After all, he knew Estelle as well as anyone. Oliver had been the one who'd first suggested the addition of a genealogical section to the library and the one who donated the first reference books. He'd also been the chief consultant on the project and had worked closely with Estelle and Delia throughout. He was wearing his smug grin, the one that was a natural outgrowth of his superiority syndrome. Delia wondered why someone didn't slap it right off his face. Then she immediately regretted the thought. She was tense, and tension always made her hostile.

German and Reb stood near the door of the church. They would be leading the procession to the cemetery and no doubt needed to be able to make a quick getaway. German appeared to be watching Pamela rather than Brother Wagoner, though. Delia wondered for the first time just what sort of relationship he had with Pamela. Now that she remembered it, he'd been especially solicitous of Pam during those dreadful moments in the library when they'd first discovered Estelle's body.

"How long is this going to last?" Roger whispered.

"Beats me. Just sit still and behave yourself," Delia ordered. She hoped, though, that the service wouldn't last much longer. Afterward they were all expected to attend a graveside ceremony, and the sky appeared to grow darker every minute. Nothing worse than rain for a funeral, Delia thought. And with the temperature dropping every day, it was bound to be a miserable mess.

Ahead of them Frankie Mae sighed loudly, indicating either extreme grief or—more likely—impatience. Frankie Mae had told several people earlier that she didn't hold with rites such as this. "Just bury 'em, for Pete's sake," she'd said. "Let the rest of us get on with it."

A sudden silence and the rustle of people emitting coughs they'd been holding in signaled that it was time for the final prayer. Delia bowed her head, hoping Roger would hold out another few minutes. His hand had strayed to her thigh and was stroking it suggestively. Delia slid her hand down to catch his and hold it captive until the prayer was over. Unfortunately Roger took that as a sign that she was as eager as he to be out of the church and into something more private. For the rest of the service they played a peculiar form of arm wrestling. Delia finally won by jabbing an elbow gently into Roger's ribs.

They drove the six miles to the cemetery in Roger's car, Delia sitting as close to the passenger door as she dared. Since the heat in Roger's car was as unpredictable as the man himself, she'd bundled herself into her coat and then wrapped herself in one of the blankets that Roger kept in the backseat.

"You could move a little closer," Roger told her several times, to which Delia replied that decorum was prescribed on a few occasions in life and this was one of them.

"Estelle would have much preferred that we all go home and leave her in peace," Roger argued.

"You sound like Frankie Mae. Believe me, Estelle would have preferred the flags flown at half-

mast and a national period of mourning. She believed in ceremony."

"I suppose you knew her better than I. It's just
that I never quite figured out what we're supposed
to do. Cry? Keen? Throw ourselves upon the funeral pyre? What?"

"Reflect, Roger. Remember all the wonderful
times with Estelle."

"I personally never had any wonderful times with
Estelle. Most of my times with Estelle were down-
right frustrating, what with my trying to check out
a particular book and her not having a clue as to
its whereabouts." Roger was driving with his left
hand and flipping the heater switch on and off and
on with his right. He believed sincerely that this
would generate warmth. He was wrong.

Delia leaned to her left and patted his leg. "All
right, dear. You've made your point. Now hush and
reflect upon the fragility of life. That should keep
you out of trouble until we can get away."

After a dusty summer, rain had finally poured
down in early autumn, ruining all chance of color-
ful foliage. The trees they now passed bore brown,
dead-looking leaves. The sky, meanwhile, had
grown darker, and a few drops of rain splatted
against the windshield. Roger and Delia were
among the last cars to reach the cemetery. From
the highway Delia could see almost nothing beyond
a sea of black umbrellas.

Taking Roger's arm for support against the
treachery of high heels on soft dirt, Delia watched
the funeral-home manager and Brother Wagoner
arrange the family and closest friends around the
coffin. She wondered if there were a particular order to be observed or if the positioning had more to

do with psychological and emotional support. If the latter, the preacher would face a real dilemma in figuring out who might be of most benefit to Walt Jr.

There were perhaps a dozen people seated underneath the green canopy that advertised (discreetly and with good taste, of course) Looby Brothers Funeral Home. Most of the mourners glanced at the darkening sky or checked their wristwatches. Again, the Leaches and Pamela were sitting in front, but now Oliver had joined them. Judging by the way Eliza was ignoring his attempts at conversation, he had not been invited to sit among the elect. Brother Wagoner stood beside the coffin, Bible in hand. Walt sat in the middle chair, seemingly unaware of anything except his mother's coffin.

Brother Wagoner waited until the last few mourners had gathered themselves into a circle around the tent, then stood and began to read the Twenty-third Psalm. " 'Surely goodness and mercy shall follow me all the days of my life: and I will dwell in the house of the Lord for ever.' "

And with that it was over. Everyone stood up and began to mill about. A few people headed straight to their cars or stopped to chat with Pamela, whose face reflected more strain than it had since the day she'd walked into the library and seen the effects of vandalism.

Walt Jr. rose solemnly and shook hands with the preacher and a few of the men standing nearest him. Eliza approached him and said something that Delia couldn't hear. Walt shook his head and started to leave. Spotting Delia, he stopped and stood in place for a minute as if trying to make a

decision. Finally he walked over to where she and
Roger stood.

"Delia," he said simply. "Thank you for coming."

"Of course, Walt. I wanted to be here." Delia
wasn't sure if she should elaborate on that sentiment or not. Was there a ritual greeting and response for gravesite encounters? For people like
Delia, who diligently avoided all but the most man-
datory funerals, the standard phrases didn't seem
enough. Yet she had never been able to devise anything better.

"I wondered . . ." Walt said, then trailed off. "I
think Mother probably has—had—a number of
books on family history. Bibles, records of one sort
or another. It may be a long time before I can manage to sort through things, but when I do . . . would
that be the kind of thing you'd need at the library?
I know Mother's mentioned a history section, Jesus
Creek history, that is."

"That's exactly the sort of contribution we'd welcome," Delia said. She didn't mean to sound so eager, but in truth she was. It had not occurred to her
until just that moment, but Estelle was a pack rat
who would have saved every relevant document,
every newspaper clipping and marriage license and
birth certificate she'd ever run across. "It would be
very kind of you to donate that."

"I'll do it then," Walt said, with a hint of a smile.
"It could be a while."

"Don't worry about the time it takes. We all understand."

"Thank you, Delia," he said simply, and walked
away toward his car. He drove around the paved
maze that surrounded the cemetery and finally onto
the highway. No one seemed to have noticed his

departure. Delia had the feeling that he'd meant to say more.

With Walt gone and the rain pouring down steadily, Delia guided Roger to the small cluster of people who still remained. "Pamela, have you considered taking a few days off? You're obviously not feeling well and—"

"No, absolutely not," Pamela assured her. "Work is just what I need."

"And of course," said Eliza, "she'll have Sarah Elizabeth to help."

Sarah Elizabeth smiled brightly, but Pamela didn't notice. She had clutched her purse to her chest and was slowly edging away from the gravesite.

"We'll give you a ride," Delia said, reaching for Pamela's arm.

Pamela jumped, apparently lost in her thoughts. "What?" she asked, trying to focus on Delia.

"I said, we'll give you a ride home. Unless you have your own car."

"No, no. I came with Eliza but—"

"Never mind, dear," Eliza said soothingly. "You go on with Delia. Might do you good to go out for lunch or something, too."

"Yes, that sounds like a good idea," Delia agreed. "Where would you like to go, Pam?"

"You're very kind, Delia, but I don't think I could. If you don't mind, I'd just like to take off. There's work to do before we open tomorrow." Pamela walked away without waiting for a reply, headed in the direction of Eliza's car.

"Not well," Eliza said. "Not at all. Keep an eye on her. She ought to take a few vacation days—or weeks. You were right about that Delia. Stubborn woman, though."

"She is that," Delia said. "For the moment I suppose we'll just have to let her ramble. When it gets to be too much for her, I expect she'll tell us."

"Yes. Or Sarah Elizabeth will notice. Good idea, that. Having Sarah Elizabeth in the library to keep an eye on things."

Eliza turned away to rejoin her family, leaving Delia and Roger free to depart. Lindsay James and Sarah Elizabeth were waiting passively for Eliza to signal that it was time for them to leave. Seeing her nod, they both headed for the car without saying goodbye to anyone.

"I'd swear Eliza uses some sort of mind control," Roger said quietly, "but I know Sarah Elizabeth is too young to have one. Does Lindsay James?"

"Not so you'd notice," Delia told him. "Pamela's doesn't seem to be in very good shape, either. She's always so . . . organized. Do you suppose she's held it in for years, just to go bonkers on us now?"

"Good point. She does look stressed, doesn't she? That surprises me." Roger took Delia's arm and led her around the headstones to the car. "I thought she didn't care that much for Estelle."

"They were like a married couple," Delia explained. "Always harping and griping. But they must have felt some affection for each other. It's difficult to work together that closely and not become attached."

"Could be," Roger said thoughtfully. "Or maybe Pamela is the one who did in Estelle."

"Roger! That's terrible."

Roger shrugged. "If you read any detective stories, you'd know that it's always the least likely character who commits the crime."

"In that case our prime suspect would be Eliza.

Can you imagine her sneaking into the library in the middle of the night and flinging books around?"

"I can imagine her doing most anything," Roger said, then stuck out his tongue at Eliza's back.

Friday morning Delia woke early. She thought about rolling over and going back to sleep. That was her favorite part of retirement. She could stay up late to read, rather than grade papers, then sleep until noon if she chose. Freedom!

But she'd promised to help out in the library for the morning hours, just until Sarah Elizabeth could get the hang of the basics. Since the basics required almost no knowledge or skill, Delia was counting on getting some of the census records transferred while there.

Delia arrived at the library a few minutes after ten. The library smelled of lemon-scented cleaning solution. The books—even on the reference shelf—looked bright and dust free. The heavy velvet drapes that had been collecting dirt and grime for years were gone and had been replaced by crisp muslin curtains. Poor Estelle would have been lost in the place.

Pamela was behind the desk, checking the morning's stack of returned books to be sure no one had tried to slip in an overdue. "We're going to have to dispense with the book-return drop," she said without looking up. "Too much damage done when people try to cram three or four books in at the same time."

"But it's so convenient."

"Not for me," Pamela said. "Needless to say, Sarah Elizabeth isn't here yet. If we get busy, you'll have to give me a hand."

"No problem," Delia assured her. "In the meantime I'll set myself up over by the genealogy section." Delia chose a chair next to the large round table and deposited her purse and coat there. She'd been transferring census information for over three months, and if no crisis arose, it was possible that she'd finish the job today.

"Good morning." Sarah Elizabeth made her entrance quietly. She'd dressed in what Delia supposed was her librarian outfit. A maroon skirt, a moss-green silk blouse, and comfortable shoes. The outfit must have been devised by Eliza. It looked far too old for Sarah Elizabeth and far less fashionable than her customary attire.

"Sarah Elizabeth," Pamela said, her mouth tight with the effort she was making not to reprimand her new assistant.

"I know I'm late, and I'm really sorry. It's a terrible way to start a new job. But Lindsay James needed me to do a few errands for him and the traffic in town is terrible."

"We're going through these cards today," Pamela said, indicating the box marked BOOKS OUT, "and calling everyone who holds an overdue book."

"I'll do that," Sarah Elizabeth offered. "Can't be too difficult, can it?" She stood in the middle of the room, looking around vaguely as if for a place to land.

"Is there a problem?" Pamela asked her.

"My purse," Sarah Elizabeth said. "Where should I put it? And my coat."

"In the office." Pamela pointed to the open office door. "There's a coatrack. Make yourself at home."

Delia suspected that the invitation had not been totally sincere. On the other hand, sometimes it was hard to tell with Pamela. She tended to sound brusque even in sentimental moments.

"Since your assistant is here, I'll get on with my census," Delia said. "Give me a shout if you need me."

"My assistant will probably be more trouble than she's worth," Pamela said under her breath.

Delia thought it best to ignore the comment. Sarah Elizabeth seemed to be a likable girl. Pamela was just out of sorts from exhaustion and shock. Most likely she wasn't thrilled about training a temporary assistant just to have Sarah Elizabeth replaced by someone permanent a few weeks later.

Delia sat down at the microfilm reader and began threading in one of the spools of film. This one contained the 1870 census for Angela County. She squinted at the screen, the spidery handwriting of some Victorian census taker weaving in and out of focus.

Delia would carefully copy all the information in order as it appeared on the census. Tonight and over the next few days she would settle in at home with coffee and a piece (or two) of applesauce cake and turn the names, now listed by district, into an alphabetical genealogist's dream, neatly typed and bound into a labeled notebook. The notebook would then be placed on the library shelves alongside others containing the census for 1840, 1850, and so on. Of course, as Pamela had pointed out any number of times, if the library were equipped with a computer, the task would be much easier.

"All set," Sarah Elizabeth said, coming back into the reading room. "Now what would you like me to do first?"

Delia noted that Pamela glanced up without

speaking. No doubt she was pondering her possible
answers. She finally settled on one. "Take over
here. These cards are books that are still out.
These"—she pointed to a handful that were held
together with a rubber band—"are all overdue. Find
out who has them. Call each and every one of these
people and explain that they must return the books,
and be sure you explain the amount of the fine."

"And how much is the fine?" Sarah Elizabeth
asked.

Pamela glared at her. "Five cents a day," she
said between clenched teeth.

"And how do I figure out who has which book?"

For a minute Delia thought Pamela might have
been pushed to the breaking point. Both hands were
clenched into fists and her face had begun to turn
bright red. Finally she said, "Never mind, Sarah
Elizabeth. I'll take care of this myself. Why don't
you go into the back and make a pot of coffee?"

"Oh. Sure thing." Sarah Elizabeth pitched the
cards onto the desk and trotted off to the back,
happy to be of help.

"Never," Pamela said quietly. "Not in a million
years will I work with that woman. I'm making an
appointment with the board right away."

"She's only temporary, Pam. Better than nothing, isn't she? Just sit tight and see what happens."
Delia, to her credit, did not suggest that Pamela
try teaching Sarah Elizabeth instead of expecting
the girl to understand the library systems instinc-
tively. Sometimes it was a good idea to keep one's
mouth shut.

Pamela might have said more, but German came
in at that moment. He bolted directly to Pamela,
his expression grim. "We've got an official report,"

he said quietly. "Nothing we didn't expect, of course. Estelle was hit on the head with something pretty heavy. The chief wouldn't tell you this, of course, but I'd say it was a hammer."

Pamela sighed and shook her head. "It's very nice of you to keep me up to date," she told German. "I gather you have no idea who's responsible."

"None. The chief thinks it was some kid who got caught trying to rip off the cash box."

Delia stood up and walked quickly over to the desk where Pamela and German were standing. "That just doesn't make sense," she said quietly. "Why would Estelle be here in the wee hours? Even if she saw someone breaking in, why didn't she just call for help?"

"Beats me," German admitted. The tobacco he was chewing seemed to be getting the better of him, and he surveyed the room for a place to spit. Finding nothing available, he took a tissue from the box on the desk and stuffed it into the Styrofoam coffee cup he'd been sipping from. "It wasn't like her to stick around the library all night, that's for damn sure." He spat.

"It certainly wasn't," Pamela agreed. "But what other explanation is there?"

German put his hand gently on her shoulder. "I want you to be careful," he said. "This may be some sort of nut we're dealing with. At no time are you to be alone in this library. Do you have an assistant yet?"

"Well, there's Sarah Elizabeth—"

"Good. If she has to leave, keep Delia. Or one of the other volunteers. But for Pete's sake, don't ever stay here alone. If anyone comes in here acting the least bit peculiar, call me right away."

"Do you think there's some sort of serial killer on the loose who murders librarians?" Delia asked. "That's sort of unlikely, isn't it?"

"Extremely unlikely," German admitted with a self-conscious grin. "But until we figure out what the hell did happen, we got to consider all the possibilities. Now promise me," he said to Pamela.

"Yes, of course. I'll be very careful," Pamela told him absently. "But I don't believe for one minute that Sarah Elizabeth would provide any protection."

"She's better than nothing," German insisted.

Pamela looked unconvinced. In fact, it occurred to Delia that if things continued the way they'd started this morning, it might be Sarah Elizabeth who wound up dead. Pamela just might kill her.

CHAPTER
7

DELIA HAD TRIED HARD TO CONCENTRATE on the census records, but the bickering that went on between Sarah Elizabeth and Pamela was impossible to ignore. It seemed that Sarah Elizabeth couldn't do anything to suit Pamela, and Pamela had grown even more intolerant than usual. The surprise of the day was that Sarah Elizabeth had begun to assert herself after the first hour or so. Delia hadn't expected it, but at least now she didn't feel quite so obligated to defend the girl herself.

Delia decided to treat herself to lunch, maybe even to a piece of chess pie for dessert. Anyone who listened to those two go at it all day deserved a break now and then.

It was barely fifty yards from the library to Eloise's Diner, but the temperature had continued its steady decline and the wind had picked up again just as Delia stepped outside. She tucked one hand into the pocket of her heavy coat and used the other to tug her stocking cap over her ears and hold it there. Leaning into the wind like a mime, she fought gusts all the way. So how was it that Miss Constance Winter could be prancing down the street like a frosty elf?

" 'Lo, Miss Constance," Delia mumbled through the scarf she'd wrapped across her lower face. "You're going to freeze out here. Why don't you come on into Eloise's with me and I'll buy you a cup of coffee."

Miss Constance shook her head. "Lordy mercy, you know I ain't got time to jaw. Why, Delia, the days are short and there's tons to do. Still got half a basket to deliver." For proof, Miss Constance held out the nearly full basket of carrot cookies she was pushing today.

"Don't you think you could take a day off now and then?" Delia asked. "I mean, when the weather's like this—"

"Bad enough, I'll say." Miss Constance looked around her as if inspecting the climate. "Strange one, too. Don't remember it ever coming so cold this early on. I tell you, this kind of bitter, they'll have a gracious plenty to bury come January. Always happens like that."

"They'll be burying me today if I don't get in out of this wind," Delia said with conviction.

"Then why are you standing around?" Miss Constance asked with genuine amazement. "Get on in there."

"You should, too," Delia advised as she started moving again toward Eloise's. "Are you sure I can't treat you to a quick lunch? Or at least coffee?"

"Don't worry about me," Miss Constance said with a backward glance. "I'm strong as a horse. Always been sturdy, don't you know?"

Her last words were almost dissolved in the blast of air that caught Delia and shoved her through the door and into Eloise's Diner.

Delia spotted Reb right away. He was seated on a tiny stool at the counter, eating chili and telling vulgar jokes to Eloise, who probably knew them all anyway.

" 'Morning, Reb," Delia said, taking the seat next to him. "Hard at it, I see."

He looked at her with alarm. "Just trying to find a little peace. You aren't here to report any more crimes, are you?"

"No, no. Just looking for peace myself. I've spent the morning in the library listening to Pamela berate Sarah Elizabeth."

"Hmmph. I heard Sarah Elizabeth is working there now. Eliza's idea, was it?"

Delia sighed. "Poor Sarah Elizabeth doesn't realize what she's gotten into, I'm afraid. She seems like a nice girl. Do you know her very well?"

"Nope," Reb said. He put a plastic package of crackers on the counter, crushed them with his hand, then opened the package and poured the crumbs into his chili. "I don't hobnob with the Leaches, Delia. You'll recall that Eliza was never one for letting down social barriers."

Delia did recall. Even as a child, Eliza had maintained a careful distance from those she had once actually referred to as her social inferiors. There was something else that Delia had just remembered, too.

"Reb, didn't you take Estelle to our senior prom?"

"I picked her up and drove her home. That's about all I did with Estelle that night."

"Oliver was talking about that the other day. I'd almost forgotten. It's been a long time, hasn't it?"

"Damned long time," Reb agreed.

"Estelle was crying in the bathroom all through the prom. Oh, it didn't have anything to do with you. She was upset about Franklin and Eliza being there together."

Reb nodded. "That's right. Estelle and Franklin had a thing going for a while back in school. Oliver was talking about that, was he? He must be desperate for dirt if he has to dig back that far."

"Actually, he implied that Estelle and Franklin were having an affair later. *After* Franklin married Eliza."

Reb shook his head. "Nope. I don't believe it for one minute. I'll grant you, I've seen Estelle throw some pretty pathetic looks at Franklin, but that was way back when. Before Walt. She wouldn't have anything to do with a married man. Just not in her nature."

"I agree. What worries me is that Oliver's speculations usually stem from something. Ordinarily he has at least a crumb of fact before he builds his theory."

"Not this time," Reb said sharply. "The library looking any better? If I were just a volunteer like you, I'd get the hell out of there until the cleanup's done."

"First of all, I'm not *just* a volunteer. Volunteers are extremely important to the library because there's more work to be done than the librarians could handle alone. And second, I can't leave because I'm in the middle of a project."

"Some people don't know when to quit." Reb

downed his iced tea and left Delia to figure out exactly what he meant.

"I saw German this morning," she said, ignoring his remark, which she understood perfectly. "He told Pamela to be extremely careful. He seems to think there's a possibility that whoever killed Estelle might be back."

"Hah!" Reb snorted. "Boy's full of it, you know? He's all fired up about us having a mur-der-er." Reb dragged the word, grinning all the while.

"You do have a murderer," Delia pointed out. "And I trust you're doing all you can to find him."

"Now, listen. I don't want people getting hysterical. This is just a single crime. Whoever killed Estelle, we're sure to find him. We've never had an unsolved murder in Jesus Creek and we aren't going to start any new trends."

"What about the time Carolyn Stuart's husband shot her boyfriend?"

"That wasn't unsolved. Thirteen people saw it happen. The only difference this time is we don't have an eyewitness. But we'll find something. Soon. So don't any of you get carried away about a lunatic who stalks librarians."

"If you're so sure of that, then why did German warn Pamela to be extra cautious?"

"Because the boy's half-stupid. That'd be my guess. Probably caused by all that jumping around he does in his karate class. Jiggles the brain." Reb pointed to his own head and crossed his eyes to demonstrate the danger.

Delia sighed. She loved Reb dearly, but damn, he irritated her sometimes. "Reb, you're not taking this quite as seriously as you should. Surely you must have some clues."

"Frankly, Delia, not a one. Unless someone comes forward with a vital piece of information, there's very little we can do." He held up one hand to stop Delia's protest. "We'll keep looking, of course. Far as I'm concerned the case won't be closed till we've found our man."

"Then why don't you put German in charge of the investigation? He's got the energy, Lord knows, and he'd probably be tickled to track down every little detail. Plus it would give him a chance to impress Pamela."

Reb looked at her thoughtfully. "Now that's not a bad idea. It'd keep the boy out of my hair. I just might do that, Delia."

"Good. At least someone will be doing something."

The town of Jesus Creek occupied two blocks along Main Street. Most of the buildings still bore the names of the original businesses from the time the town was incorporated in 1840, with only a few minor changes on the facades. The courthouse stood on a grassy square in the middle of them all, so that it was possible to walk the entire town and around the court square in less than five minutes. In decent weather it was also possible to take one's time, observe a game of checkers being played on the courthouse lawn, stroll through the miniature memorial park, buy vegetables from Mennonite peddlers in front of the movie house, or sit on the steps of Marion's Dance Studio (formerly Hansen's Feed and Grain) and watch motorists ignore the town's only traffic light.

Feeling renewed after her cheese sandwich and salad, Delia decided to make one quick stop before returning to the census rolls. She needed a couple of folders and a ream of paper before she started transferring the records, and Leach Print Shop and Office Supply was just two doors down from the diner, on the corner of Main Street and Morning Glory Way. This was also the home of Jesus Creek's weekly newspaper, *The Headlight*, the pride of Lindsay James Leach, owner, publisher, and editor.

The front portion of the office was set off by a high counter. This was officially the office supply. Behind the counter there existed the mysterious print shop, which Delia had never had the privilege of visiting. She'd heard strange sounds and unidentifiable smells coming from that direction and had often reminded herself to ask Lindsay James for a tour. She was sure he'd love showing off his skill and knowledge about the only subject on which anyone considered him an authority.

This morning there was no one behind the register, but as soon as the door slammed shut, jingling its warning bell, Delia heard Kay's voice. "Coming!"

Kay Martin came around the counter at a jog and smiled broadly when she saw her customer. "Delia! Hi there!" Kay was wearing a sweater and denim skirt, with something that looked like plow boots on her feet. No one had ever said that Kay was fashionable, but they couldn't deny that she was her own person when it came to style. "Sorry. We're one short today and I'm trying to do both jobs."

"Someone sick?" Delia asked.

Kay leaned over the bulky, almost antique cash register. "Someone terminated," she whispered. "You remember Ernie Odle?"

Delia nodded. Ernie was the shifty-eyed employee who probably dipped into the till. Or so Delia had decided after their first and only meeting.

"When Mrs. Wilby didn't get her gossip column—excuse me, her local news—in on time, Lindsay James told Ernie to call her and check on it. Well, you know how cranky Mrs. Wilby is?"

Delia nodded again.

"Ernie didn't call. He just ran one of her columns from last year."

"You're kidding!" Delia said. "I didn't even notice."

"Nobody but Lindsay James did. And he raised three kinds of hell before he fired Ernie. L.J.'s touchy about journalistic integrity."

Just then Lindsay James peeked over the dividing counter. " 'Morning, Delia," he said, and returned to the back without waiting for her to reply.

"I must have caught you in the middle of printing day," Delia said.

"That was yesterday," Kay explained, rubbing at the ink splotch across her nose. Since her fingers were black, too, she did more damage than repair, but Kay didn't seem to notice. "Today we're collating. Sticking all those sale papers in your news. You know, the ones you're going to throw away without reading? But the advertisers pay us to do it. Hey, money's money."

"You're worldy-wise for one so young," Delia said.

"That's how I got where I am today. Can I help you find something, or are you just browsing?" It was known to all the print-shop employees that Delia Cannon could spend hours browsing through the place, looking at paper and pens and rubber-band holders and all the seductive things that an office supply had to offer.

"I'd love to look," Delia said wistfully. "But I have to get back to the library. I'm doing census. Today I'm only allowing myself two folders and a ream of paper."

"Okay. I'll get the paper from the back while you find your folders." Kay was gone and back by the time Delia had found just the folders she wanted. "You're into that genealogy stuff, aren't you?"

"Right. But don't worry. I won't bore you with all the details of my illustrious ancestors." Delia pulled her wallet from her purse and waited for Kay to total the bill. "Shoot, I'm probably the only person you'll ever meet who doesn't have a Cherokee princess grandmother to brag about."

"I wish Oliver Host was more like you. That's all?"

"That's it," Delia said, and counted out a few bills.

"He never shuts up. Would you believe, when I was doing the layout for his book, he came in here at least twice a week to see what I'd done? Then he'd make changes. I didn't think we'd ever get that sucker finished."

"Oh, you printed his book? Well, I guess that makes sense. I just hadn't thought about it."

"Oh, yes. We printed it. And now we're going to have to do it again because all the copies got burned in the fire. Let me tell you, honey, *I* won't be doing it this time. Lindsay James can deal with the old goat."

"Well, I hope Lindsay James gets on the ball. I'm eager to see Oliver's book, and he won't sell me the one copy he's got left."

"You want a copy?" Kay looked up at Delia and rolled her big brown eyes. "Why?"

"Because there's a chance that Oliver has really pieced together some interesting local history."

"No, there's not. I've read it and proofread it and read it again. But if you really think you can stand it . . ." Kay knelt behind the register and stood up with a copy of Oliver's book in her hands.

"Where'd you get this?" Delia asked, amazed.

"We always have an overrun. Just in case of blurred print or something. We've got about ten down here. I was going to throw them out the other day, but I just didn't get to it. Here, you can have this. Don't tell Oliver, though."

"I'll never breathe a word. Bless your heart, kiddo."

"I'll give you the rest if you promise to come in and do the next printing for him."

"That's okay," Delia said, and winked. "I've put up with Oliver longer than you have. There's a limit to how much of him a person should have to bear."

Now that she had *The History of the Original Families of Jesus Creek*, Delia wanted to plunge into it rather than return to the glare of the microfilm reader. She promised herself a wonderful dinner and an evening of Oliver's book, which somehow didn't seem to appease her stomach.

When she returned reluctantly to the library, Sarah Elizabeth and Pamela were still arguing.

"Not there," Pamela was saying. "That's a nine hundred. Pay attention to the number, Sarah Elizabeth."

"It says eight-thirty," Sarah Elizabeth replied stubbornly.

"Nonsense." Pamela grabbed the book from Sarah Elizabeth's hand and studied the number stuck to its spine.

"See?" Sarah Elizabeth said petulantly.

"Well, obviously Estelle numbered it wrong. You can't go by the numbers alone, Sarah Elizabeth. You'll have to check the title. If that doesn't convey anything, you might try opening the book to discover the subject."

"And you might have told me that when we started. How was I supposed to know you people had numbered the books wrong?"

"I certainly didn't do it. Estelle, however, was never very conscientious. You'll have to watch for her mistakes," Pamela said, then added, "as well as watching for your own."

"I've almost finished here," Delia said quickly. "After I transfer this last census, I think I'll go on home. That is, if there's nothing you need me for."

"Fine," Pamela said sharply. "Nothing is getting accomplished today, anyway."

Sarah Elizabeth rolled the book cart smoothly to the shelves at the far end of the room and pretended not to have heard.

"This isn't going to work," Pamela said deliberately. "The girl is a fool."

"Shhh. Give it time," Delia told her. "You can't expect her to learn everything in one day."

"At this point, I don't expect her to learn anything at all. She has absolutely no understanding of the Dewey decimal system. She can't seem to retain anything I tell her—"

"She's only been here a day, Pamela."

"Well, perhaps that's the problem. If she'd spent any time in a library, even as a patron, she'd be at least mildly familiar with the procedure."

"Sarah Elizabeth majored in library science in school. She obviously has some passing acquaintance with libraries or she wouldn't have chosen that for her career."

"Career, my hind end. Surely, Delia, you're aware of the age-old tradition. Sarah Elizabeth went to college to find a husband. It hardly mattered what she majored in, since she had no intention of graduating."

Delia thought Pamela might have an outdated notion of coeducation. After all, most women nowadays were career oriented, weren't they? "Well, I'm sure she'll learn soon enough. And if she doesn't, the board will find someone suitable."

"Assuming the board ever does anything. They should have called an emergency meeting right after Estelle's death."

"Give it time, Pamela. I'm sure they'll attend to it." Delia wasn't half as confident as she sounded, however. It had occurred to her that Eliza was on the board. The other members were her friends, and they, like everyone else, were terrified of Eliza. It was just possible that Eliza intended a permanent position for her daughter-in-law. In any case she would be completely oblivious to Pamela or Sarah Elizabeth's wishes.

Delia settled in at her desk and ran a roll of microfilm through the machine. Was it possible, she wondered, that Eliza intended to do just that? Sarah Elizabeth might have been railroaded into a job she didn't want for purely ulterior reasons. For that matter, could Estelle have been killed for her job?

But who would want it? The board had hired Pamela, an out-of-towner, as a last resort when they couldn't find a Jesus Creek resident qualified or willing to accept the position of assistant librarian. Who, other than Pamela herself, would have wanted the head librarian's job?

Delia knew she was getting carried away. The truth was probably that Eliza wanted to get Sarah Elizabeth out of her hair for a few hours every day. Or perhaps she was living vicariously through her new daughter-in-law. Eliza herself had never worked outside the home, but she'd pretty much run the family business from behind the scenes, first by completely subjugating her husband, then her son.

The trouble was, Eliza had never encountered anyone in Jesus Creek quite like Pamela Satterfield. Pamela was an outsider, someone whose family had not lived in Jesus Creek for three or four generations. While Delia and the rest of the natives gave Eliza a wide berth and even pretended to abide her delusions of grandeur (Delia supposed they were all pretending, anyway), someone like Pamela might not understand the rules. Then again, maybe Pamela understood the rules perfectly and intended to break them. The resultant confrontation between Eliza and Pamela could make for riveting melodrama—just so long as Delia stayed back far enough to avoid the splattered blood.

CHAPTER
8

ROGER WAS PUTTERING AROUND IN HER kitchen when Delia finally arrived home. She dumped her armload of census records on the desk in the living room and peeked around the doorway. Roger was wearing one of her aprons and standing over a steaming pot of soup. He looked pretty sexy in ruffles, Delia noted.

"Dinner is served," he said. "Broccoli soup and fresh wheat bread, which I made my very own self while waiting for the love of my life to come home."

"There's a reason I keep you around," she told him. "You're the best little wife a woman could have." Stripping off her jacket and tossing it across the hook by the back door, Delia settled in at the small table. Roger had already arranged bowls and glasses, so that Delia had to search for an open place to prop up Oliver's book. "Look what I found," she said.

Roger ladled out soup for both of them, then

leaned over to read the title. "Good grief, woman. Must you?"

"I thought we'd read it during dinner. Who knows? Our own illustrious ancestors may be immortalized."

"Not mine, honeychile. Even if they are, I'd rather not know. Family obligation would force me to confront Oliver and challenge him to a duel. But we probably should find out. With any luck I'll be able to sue." Roger was a native of Chattanooga, that extraordinarily beautiful area in the eastern part of the state. Unfortunately it was eastern Tennessee that had not only formed a militia to oppose Confederate forces but had also threatened secession from the state—if the state seceded from the Union.

"You might rate a paragraph," Delia said casually. "I understand there's a chapter about the offspring of traitorous Yankee sympathizers."

"I won't be there either. The Yankees disowned me when I started fooling around with you."

"That's a point in your favor," Delia said, and opened the book. "Isn't this just precious? Oliver's written the entire history of his own family and put it right here at the beginning."

Delia turned past the foreword to Chapter One and began to read. " 'By the early 1800s,' " she began, and skipped the next few paragraphs. She was not interested in limestone deposits anyway. A few pages later she found the first reference to actual human beings.

" 'Palimo Leach, born 1801, was one of the first to settle in the valley. He was a skilled carpenter and soon amassed a modest fortune because he was the only carpenter within several hundred miles.

Palimo married Sarah Cumming, born 1800, and they had fourteen children before Sarah's death. (See pedigree charts at end of volume.)' There should be a better name for those charts. This makes us all sound like terriers, doesn't it?"

"Fourteen?" Roger carefully removed the frilly apron and seated himself beside Delia, pulling his chair closer to hers so that he could read over her shoulder.

"We won't bother to check the appendix just now. It's obvious to me that Palimo was some ancestor of Eliza's husband and that he had absolutely no consideration for his wife. No doubt Oliver would get the family members correct if for no other reason than to avoid Eliza's wrath."

Delia continued to scan quietly. Her hopes for discovering fascinating material were repeatedly dashed. "The next page goes on about Palimo's contributions to the community, such as land donation for the building of a church. Palimo also served as the first sheriff of the area. Eliza has never seemed particularly fond of law enforcement officers. I gather she considers them just a step above child molesters and graverobbers."

"Perhaps the job carried more prestige back in the nineteenth century," Roger suggested.

"Perhaps. 'James Leach, born 1837, was the son of Palimo and Sarah Cumming Leach,' according to page fifteen. 'He married Priscilla Kelly, born 1845, in the fall of 1860, but the marriage was not recorded until January 1861. By this time James had enlisted in the Confederate army and was serving in Maney's Battery.' "

Delia skimmed through the interminable lists of children and their spouses, through good deeds and service to the community. Surely no one would ever question the importance of the Leach family to Jesus Creek's growth and progress. It was unfortunate that the family had lost almost all of their fortune by war's end, as had many others.

"Page eighteen" she said, "explains how the Leaches regained their fortune. By marrying the wealthy Wilsons. 'Quentin Wilson, born 1803, married his cousin Elizabeth. Of their ten children only one son was born to carry on the name.'"

"Do you mean to tell me," Roger asked, "that if not for this one child, there'd be no Eliza in Jesus Creek today? My, it sends chills through me."

"Don't be sarcastic, dear," Delia told him. " 'John Wilson was born in 1836 before the tragedy of war struck his family and took from them all that they had attained.' "

"Spare me the violins."

Delia gave him a significant glance and he shut up. " 'In 1862 John married Mary Turner, daughter of a neighbor. Although Mary was barely seventeen and John already twenty-six, it was a fortuitious match, for the two families together owned most of the land in the district.' "

"And so on," Delia muttered, stifling a yawn. Oliver's prose style was taking its toll. " 'Shortly after the marriage, John left to fight for the Confederate cause, leaving young Mary to run the plantation. She being an intelligent and capable woman, the family fortune flourished. But later that year, tragedy struck the family when John was killed at the Battle of Stone's River.

" 'This might have been the end of the Wilson family name, but on 21 October 1863 Mary gave birth to Zithius Wilson, Eliza's grandfather and John Wilson's only heir.' "

Delia skimmed the rest of the page and summarized for Roger, who was starting to make faces at her. "It seems that the next generation saw the intertwining of the Leach family with all its noble deeds and the Wilson family, whose land holdings and finances had grown considerably under the young widow Mary's guidance. Three cheers for women's lib." Delia raised her cup in a silent salute to Mary Wilson.

"Yes, indeed. Now"—Roger reached across the table and gently took the book away from her—"how are you, my dear? Tell me everything about your life."

"Roger, for heaven's sake. What's gotten into you? Are you trying to butter me up?" Delia stared at him, hoping to frighten him into a confession of whatever sin he'd committed. "What have you done?"

"I'm just trying to be nice. Really, you are a suspicious woman." Roger buttered a piece of bread and ate it thoughtfully, wearing his studied look of innocence.

"You're up to something. Let's have it, darlin'. What's going on?"

"Nothing at all. I swear. Now eat your dinner." Roger pointed his spoon at her bowl. "It's good for you. A woman of your age should not neglect nutrition."

"I expect you're right. I have to work hard to keep up with all those young studs in my life." Delia smiled sweetly and ate.

* * *

Delia spent Friday evening organizing and typing the census records for 1870 and 1880. At first it hadn't been easy to persuade Roger to go home, but he'd finally admitted his apathy toward the transfer of census records.

It was already dark outside by the time she had tucked the records into neatly labeled folders. Tomorrow when she did her shopping, she'd drop them off at the library. Ordinarily the library would not open on Saturday, but Pamela had insisted on it. She'd said there was entirely too much chaos among the shelves to take a day off. There was a mild possibility that Sarah Elizabeth would have resigned by then and Delia wouldn't have to listen to all that bickering.

Stretching her arms over her head and rotating gently at the waist, she tried to work out the kinks in her back that had been caused by sitting all day. She'd decided to phone Eliza and find out if the board had set about hiring a permanent replacement for Estelle. When Eliza answered on the second ring, Delia started by asking after Sarah Elizabeth.

"She's getting the hang of things at the library," Eliza replied. "No thanks to that Satterfield woman. She's making life very difficult for Sarah Elizabeth. After all, it's a new experience for her. Entering the workplace, that is."

"Yes, I expect so," Delia said. "Pamela is still on edge and she may resent having someone, *anyone*, working there in Estelle's place. But Sarah Elizabeth will catch on. She's bright."

"I'll have a talk with Pamela about it," Eliza went on. "Unless you'd care to do it. As a board member, Pamela might feel that my suggestions are . . . well, a sort of reprimand. And we don't want to ruffle her feathers, do we?"

Hah, Delia thought. "Maybe we should just leave it to the two of them. I'm sure Sarah Elizabeth will get more comfortable as she goes along."

"No doubt. She's quite determined. As I told you, she had intended to take a degree in library science. You know, I firmly believe that a woman should have a career. It gives her an opportunity to fulfill her own ambitions."

"Apparently that attitude runs in your family. I was just reading about your great-grandmother, Mary Turner Wilson, in Oliver's book."

"Really?" Eliza said. "I understood that all those books had burned."

"I got this one on the black market," Delia said lightly. "Mary was a scrapper, wasn't she?"

"No doubt," Eliza said, awaiting further elaboration from Delia before placing an end to the pregnant pause.

"Well," Delia said, "I was wondering if the board plans to meet soon. About Estelle's replacement."

"We'll discuss the matter at our next meeting. There's no reason to call a special, not as long as Sarah Elizabeth is available."

"Ah. And that would be . . . when?"

"Another month, I believe." Clearly Eliza didn't see the situation as urgent.

"I see," Delia responded, with trepidation creeping into her voice.

"While I have you on the phone, Delia, I must ask a favor. Our speaker for the SDC meeting has canceled on us. Is there any chance that you could put together a little program?"

"No," Delia said too quickly. "I mean, I'm afraid

I just don't have the time between now and Monday night. But I'm sure you'll find someone. In the meantime give Sarah Elizabeth my best."

"I'll do that. Sarah Elizabeth will probably want to have lunch with you soon. And perhaps you can give her some moral support. Especially since it won't be forthcoming from Pamela."

"I'll do what I can, Eliza," Delia promised. She hung up wondering what she could possibly explain to Sarah Elizabeth. Delia herself knew very little about the library. Her tasks as volunteer were simple ones—phoning people with overdue books, tidying up now and then. She wondered if Sarah Elizabeth could be persuaded to become a volunteer instead of an employee. Maybe she could supervise the weekly story hour for children. Sarah Elizabeth was young enough to relate to the kids and she'd probably enjoy working with them. Delia had already decided, in one of the snap judgments she was famous for, that Sarah Elizabeth was going to make a fine mother. And she didn't think that about just anyone.

She took Oliver's book to bed with her, fully expecting to fall asleep after only a few pages. But the sight of her own name in print captured Delia's attention. It wasn't Delia herself that Oliver had immortalized—she was just a number on one of the charts tucked away in the appendix—but her many-times-great-grandmother, who had arrived with those other settlers.

Their names would not have been the same, of course, if the current Delia hadn't reclaimed hers after the divorce. As the only child of the last male Cannon, she'd felt a bit obligated. She'd planned to

stick her only child with the middle name Cannon
but old Whatshisname had refused to go along.
Probably just as well, Delia realized now. Charlotte
despised anything that smacked of originality.

The real motivation for changing her name back
to Cannon, though, was less admirable but infi-
nitely more practical. For almost seventeeen years
Delia had cringed every time she spoke the name
Delia Dandler. It sounded like a new hamburger
chain.

Charlotte had suffered through the last two years
of high school trying to avoid introducing her
mother to anyone. She had been embarrassed by
the divorce, mortified when she had to explain why
her mother was a Cannon and she was a Dandler.

Delia smiled when she saw how deftly Oliver had
skipped over the history of her family. The original
Delia was a requisite entry, however, because after
the death of Mr. Cannon, she'd sold the family farm,
taken her family of nine sons into town, and established one of the first thriving businesses in Jesus
Creek. Court records from the period indicated that
Delia's Tavern had been the scene of numerous
brawls and outright homicides.

After the two short paragraphs about the Cannon
legacy, Oliver simply referred interested readers to
the completed family trees in the appendix. Delia
was not an interested reader. It had taken less than
two chapters to assure her that Oliver had failed to
unearth any new information.

Snapping off the light, Delia snuggled into bed.
For most of the night she dreamed of Oliver Host
being lynched outside a saloon full of cheering Can-
nons.

CHAPTER
9

SATURDAY WAS THE PRINCIPAL MARKET-
ing day in Jesus Creek. Ordinarily at this time of
year the weather might run to the high fifties, certainly no lower than forty. But the cold front that
had moved in a week before seemed to have settled
permanently over the area. Today it was bitter
enough to keep all but the most desperate shopper
at home.

Delia was wearing insulated boots, two pairs of
socks, thermal underwear, slacks, a flannel shirt, a
sweater, a long coat, mittens, a scarf, and a stocking cap. It was practically her entire winter wardrobe and it still wasn't enough to ward off the cold.
By her second trip around the court square, she was
thinking seriously of giving up exercise until
spring.

"Delia, you'd better stand up straight or your
backbone will grow that way!" Miss Constance was
just coming out of Pate's Hardware across the

street. Her coat was unbuttoned and she had only
a straw hat tied on with a gauzy pink scarf.

"Can't help it!" Delia called back. "Cold!"

Miss Constance waved her off, as if disgusted by
Delia's susceptibility to frostbite.

Gathering the last of her rapidly deteriorating
energy, Delia broke into a run and headed for
Eloise's Diner. It was times like this when she
wished she hadn't forsaken meat. A nice hot steak
would . . . no, she wouldn't think about it. "Slaugh-
tered animals," she mumbled, and pictured an ab-
attoir scene as she burst through the door of the
diner.

Even with the heat turned up full blast, Eloise's
was cool. Several customers were still wearing hats
and coats while eating breakfast or drinking coffee.

Oliver Host and Reb Gassler were sitting in the
far corner booth. Oliver was talking and gesturing
with his fork, occasionally looking up to bestow a
smile on one or another of the customers. Reb was
completely involved in the monumental breakfast
in front of him.

Delia sighed. She knew Reb was a big boy. She
knew that there was absolutely no reason why she
shouldn't take a seat at the counter and enjoy her
breakfast. She also knew that she was going to
march right over there and rescue Reb.

"Good morning," she said, as cheerfully as her
cold-numbed lips would allow.

"Delia!" Reb said, more enthusiastically than the
simple greeting would have conveyed under other
circumstances. The relief in his voice made Delia
feel guilty that she'd even considered leaving him
to his fate. "Sit here."

"Thanks, Reb," Delia said. She reluctantly removed her coat and draped it over a hook by the booth.

"You're here for breakfast?" Oliver asked with a smirk. "I thought Roger did the cooking at your place."

"Generally he does," Delia said, and flashed him a killer smile. "And it's always wonderful. You know, to find a man with enough intelligence to operate a stove is quite a bit of luck." There. Let the woefully unskilled Mr. Host choke on that.

Oliver seemed unaware of the implication. "But he isn't in the mood this morning, is that it?"

"Roger is on his way to Nashville," Delia explained. "He's warming up for the big race later this week."

"Still playing with those little cars, huh?" Reb found the idea of a grown man racing slot cars wildly amusing.

Delia had once tried to explain to Reb how difficult it was to build an engine the size of a matchbox and how one's reflexes had to be finely tuned to race the little devils. Unfortunately she didn't know much about Roger's hobby. She'd gone along once to watch him race and had suffered from stiff muscles for days afterward. Not wanting to embarrass herself or Roger, she'd restrained herself even though every cell in her body had wanted to jump up and down and scream encouraging words to make the cars go faster. Apparently sitting demurely in a corner had been more strenuous than physical activity.

"I'll buy you breakfast," Reb offered. "Maybe while Shelton's away, I can get you to play with me."

"Roger wouldn't appreciate that," Oliver said. He was smirking again.

Eloise arrived to take her order before Delia could explain that her life was her own and Roger did not tell her who she could play with. Not that she'd have tried explaining anything like that to Oliver. Any conversation with him was bound to degenerate into a dueling match, with Delia on the defensive, if she attempted to straighten his warped idea of male-female relationships.

She ordered coffee and a blueberry muffin, then turned to Reb. "Have you learned anything new about Estelle's death?"

"Looks like someone used a hammer on her," Reb said, and slugged down the last of his coffee. He didn't seem to notice that Delia flinched. "Probably the same hammer that was used to break the glass in the back door. Kinda stupid, if you ask me. Lot of noise."

"I think you're looking at it from a purely subjective point of view," Oliver observed. He leaned back in his chair, prepared to pontificate. "Perhaps the intruder had a very specific reason for choosing the hammer over another weapon."

"Yeah?" Reb lifted an eyebrow. "Like what?"

"I can think of several explanations," Oliver said, and checked his watch. "But I haven't the time for details. I'm sure you'll be able to come up with something if you try." Oliver rose and collected his overcoat from the rack behind them, carefully checking it for wrinkles before putting it on. "I'm on a strict schedule. There are a few updates to be included in my book before the next printing."

"When will that be?" Delia asked.

"I don't have an exact date," Oliver said vaguely. "It's been nice chatting with you, Delia. Reb."

As Oliver headed across the room toward the cash register Reb mumbled, "Chatting *at* us, he means. Just about ruined my breakfast."

"Why didn't you tell him to scat?" Delia asked.

"I did. He just kept sitting here and yakking about that book. You ever notice how some people can't be insulted?"

Delia nodded. "It's a serious character flaw."

"And I'd like to know where he learned to talk like that. Not around here, that's for sure."

It was true that somewhere along the way, Oliver had lost all trace of his Tennessee accent. Like Reb and Delia and the rest, Oliver had lived his whole life in Jesus Creek, except for those few years at college. Even then he'd returned home almost every weekend to visit his mother.

"Hmmph," Reb said, and pointed toward the front of the diner. "Looks like Oliver caught another victim."

Delia turned halfway around in her chair to look. Lindsay James had come in to pick up several cups of coffee for the newspaper staff. "Coffeepot over at the office burned out," he was explaining to Eloise. "Somebody left it turned on all night."

"That's very dangerous," Oliver told him. "Could have started a fire, you know. It should be your responsibility to check those things before you leave for the night."

Lindsay James said something that Delia couldn't hear. He was digging bills out of his wallet, trying hard not to look at Oliver. Maybe he thought ignoring Oliver would cause him to disappear, or at

least to shut up. Lindsay James should have known
better.

"Still," Oliver went on, "as owner and manager,
it *is* your responsibility, Lindsay James. Anything
less would be shirking your duty, wouldn't it? Almost like deserting your appointed post?"

Lindsay James put money on the counter and
turned away, nearly knocking over a chair in his
attempt to flee. Behind him, Oliver smirked.

"That would be Oliver's publisher," Delia explained.

"Yeah," Reb said. "Everybody knows that. Except Oliver."

Eloise delivered Delia's muffin and coffee, then
cleared the dishes left by Oliver. She glanced discreetly under the saltshaker and napkin holder for
a tip. There was none. "And his daddy was a bach-
elor, too," Eloise mumbled as she collected Oliver's
used dishes.

"Walt Jr.'s coming in to pack up Estelle's stuff,"
Reb said. "He's pretty upset. Doesn't show it
much."

"He never did. Walt's a lot like his father. *He*
never changed expressions, either."

"Except for that goofy grin he wore the day he
married Estelle." Reb shook his head. "Maybe the
Carhart men are so quiet because they're always
confused. Living with Estelle would do that."

"Could be." Delia broke off pieces of muffin and
chewed them thoughtfully. "Did you ever notice
how much Walt Sr. and Franklin James resembled
one another? For that matter, Walt Jr. and Lindsay
James could be brothers. All these quiet, devoted
men." Delia sighed. "I should've had a son."

"You got problems with Charlotte?" Reb asked. "I thought she was happily married."

"She is. But she doesn't approve of me. She's always harping about my friends, my bohemian lifestyle—what?"

Reb was laughing. "Didn't we have this same conversation back when you were seventeen? You were dating Toby Milford, who had a hairdo just like Paul McCartney's and your parents didn't approve of Toby or your friends or your life-style."

"Oh, my God," Delia groaned. She'd just seen the light. "My daughter is exactly like my mother."

"I guess that's what our parents meant when they threatened that we'd pay for our raising."

Delia nodded. "I guess so. Lord knows, Charlotte has put me through the wringer."

"Sorta makes me glad I never had kids." Reb pushed back his chair. "I'll pay for breakfast and give you a ride home."

Outside the sky was still gray, the wind was still gusting. The temperature seemed to have dropped ten degrees since sunrise. Delia sat huddled in the front seat of the patrol car while Reb revved the engine to get the heater primed.

Across the street Miss Constance Winter was dropping cookie crumbs for the birds around the war memorial. The memorial was actually a standard headstone, erected on the courthouse square and engraved with the names of the Jesus Creek boys who'd died in twentieth-century wars. (Confederate victims were immortalized on a large granite slab on the other side of the courthouse.)

There were no names to mark the horror of Vietnam. Reb Gassler was the only Jesus Creek participant in that one. He'd been a corporal at the time he was discharged. Delia knew, because his mother had run an invitation to his homecoming party in the newspaper. Reb himself never mentioned his years in the service.

"Miss Constance doesn't seem bothered by the cold," Delia said. She could see her own breath inside the car.

"Hell of an old woman," Reb said. "I always heard her daddy was the real nut of the family, though. You remember him?"

Delia shook her head.

"Me either. Miss Constance must be in her eighties. Remember how she used to stand outside the school when we were kids and give us cookies during recess?"

"She still does. My classes always looked forward to it. I guess at that age none of us considered what the ingredients might be. I hate to imagine what we might have been eating."

"Didn't hurt us," Reb said. "Kind of a nice tradition, if you ask me. Kids don't have many of 'em these days."

"Yes, but at her age, it can't last much longer. The tradition can't last."

"None of 'em ever do," Reb said. The heater was finally blowing warm air. "This is a damned crazy winter, I'll tell you. Weatherman says it'll get down below zero tonight. Roger gonna be back in time to keep you warm?"

"If not, I have a lot of quilts," Delia told him.

"I guess that's better than nothing." Reb eased the car out into the nearly deserted Main Street. He cruised slowly, looking constantly from left to right and glancing into the rearview mirror.

Reb wouldn't need quilts to keep him warm tonight, of that Delia was certain. He'd been married once, just after high school, but the army had needed him more than Marie had. By the time Reb returned to Jesus Creek he wasn't interested in rejoining his friends or his wife for beer-filled nights at the Drink Tank.

After the divorce there had been a succession of women in Reb's life, all of them older and most of them single. Apparently they all understood and agreed to Reb's rules, for every woman he'd been with still adored the man.

Delia looked over at him as he pulled the patrol car into her driveway. "Thanks for the lift. If I invite you in, will you promise to behave yourself?"

"Hell, Dee, you ask a lot. I guess we'd better not take any chances. I'll just leave you here and drive off alone, into the cold lonely morning."

"Bull," Delia said, and got out of the car. She hurried toward the porch, then stood watching as Reb backed out of the driveway and headed down the one-way street. She'd known all along that he wouldn't come in.

Saturday afternoon was slow and lazy. Delia turned the electric heat to a decadent seventy-eight degrees then built a fire in the fireplace. With hot cocoa and a slice of Roger's bread she settled on the sofa to watch the never-ending string of home-repair and cooking programs on PBS while waiting for the latest installment of *Black Adder*. It would have been a perfect day to spend with Roger; in a way, though, Delia was glad he wasn't there. She felt melancholy, probably because Reb had reminded her of Toby Milford.

After she'd stopped dating Toby (okay, after Toby

had dumped her) he'd gone off to California to play
drums with a rock group called the Krickets. The
group had never made a record, so far as Delia
knew, and several years later Toby had been killed
by a hit-and-run driver. There had been rumors that
Toby had thrown himself in front of the car after
proclaiming to bystanders that he had discovered
the secret of kryptonite.

The mailman brought two bills and a note from
Margaret Jane Matthews, postmarked North Da-
kota. Margaret had heard about Estelle's death (the
note didn't say how) and hoped Delia would pass
her condolences to Estelle's family. It was signed
M.J. Obviously Margaret's gossip network was out
of touch. Estelle had no family except for Walt Jr.,
and he'd probably never heard of Margaret Jane
Matthews. Margaret had deserted the Jesus Creek
circle, so now an ink blot covered her name in the
community Bible.

Delia reached for the phone and dialed Eliza's
number. She wondered if Eliza, too, had heard from
Margaret.

"Leach residence," Eliza said briskly.

"It's Delia."

"How are you?" Eliza sounded as if she were
reading from a script and doing it perfunctorily.

Her lack of interest caused Delia to consider re-
vealing the truth about how she was, starting with
Toby Milford's Beatles haircut and working her
way through the twenty-nine years since. Instead
she told Eliza about the note from Margaret.

"Who?" Eliza asked, with obvious disinterest.

"Margaret Matthews. She was your best friend
for years."

"Of course," Eliza said. "She's well, I suppose."

"I suppose. She's heard about Estelle and wants me to give her love to the family."

"Kind of her," Eliza said. There was a distinct note of sarcasm in her voice.

"And how are you?"

"Fine. Delia, I'm really busy right now. I'm working on my speech for Monday."

"Oh, you've decided to do the program yourself?" Delia was mildly alarmed. Eliza had presented programs at three of the last four SDC meetings, each one less interesting than the last.

"My *candidate's* speech," Eliza said with some exasperation.

Of course. Estelle had been president of the SDC for four years. There was still a year left in the term, so Estelle's death would make a special election necessary. Eliza had been waiting all her life for her chance. It had looked promising for her four years ago when the last of the older generation, Olivia Host, had died and left a vacancy for some of the younger members. By a fluke, Estelle had been elected instead. For the next three meetings Eliza had been absent, claiming prior engagements. Now Eliza could run again, and a special vote would be taken at the beginning of the December meeting.

"I won't keep you, then," Delia said. "But I'd like to leave a message for Sarah Elizabeth. We'd talked about having lunch, but I don't know when she has her day off. Do you?"

"I believe it's Tuesday," Eliza said. "But I'm sure she can take time for lunch any day."

"Generally they eat at the library. I don't think Pamela is going to be as flexible as Estelle was."

Did Eliza snort? Delia wondered. Surely not.

"Pamela Satterfield has very little to say about such matters. Just tell me when you want to meet Sarah Elizabeth and I'll give her the message."

"Let's make it Tuesday, then," Delia said. "At my house."

"Very well. If that's all, I have to get back to work." Eliza didn't wait to find out if that was all, but hung up abruptly.

Roger called at two A.M. to let Delia know he'd arrived home safely and would be on her doorstep bright and early Sunday morning.

"You could've waited until dawn to tell me that," Delia said groggily.

"I wanted you to sleep soundly. I know how you worry, tossing and turning whenever I'm away. Tomorrow I'll come over and we'll take the phone off the hook. Then we'll spend the day doing wonderful things to each other."

Roger turned out to be an excellent prophet.

CHAPTER
10

ROGER HAD INSISTED ON ACCOMPANYING Delia to the SDC meeting. She insisted that he'd be sorry, but he had heard through the grapevine that she could bring a guest and he seemed determined. Well, he couldn't say he hadn't been warned.

Eliza opened the meeting by walking confidently to the front of the school cafeteria and rapping her knuckles on the table.

"Can everyone hear me?" she called out. When no one answered, she assumed they could hear just fine. "Before we begin the meeting tonight, there's an important item to be discussed. As you all know, our president, Estelle Carhart, passed away recently. The constitution of the SDC states that in this or a similar event, a new president shall be chosen by special election, said president to fulfill a complete term."

Eliza looked around the room to see if everyone understood. "I propose that all candidates declare themselves during tonight's meeting in anticipa-

tion of a special election to be held at the regular
meeting next month. Is there a second?" There
was a moment of suspenseful silence as the assem-
bly waited for someone to assume the heavy responsibility of seconding. Finally Frankie Mae said,
"Second, damn it!"

"Very well. The motion has been made and sec-
onded." Eliza shuffled her note cards before going
on. "At this time I would like to declare my candidacy for president of the Sons and Daughters of the
Confederacy."

There was a smattering of applause, led by Sarah
Elizabeth and Lindsay James. Delia guessed they'd
been rigorously coached.

"Thank you," Eliza said with as much humility
as she'd ever shown. "And now let us get directly
to the business of the evening. Our speaker tonight
is known to us all, of course. Oliver Host has gra-
ciously agreed to substitute for the scheduled guest,
who, unfortunately, couldn't be here."

Roger groaned quietly, then whispered to Delia,
"You could have warned me."

"Serves you right," Delia whispered back.

Oliver had taken his place behind the speaker's
table. He did not use notes.

"I'm sure you are all familiar with the Battle of
Stone's River," he began, "but I hope to present a
few of the fascinating details of that battle that may
not be common knowledge."

Delia noticed that Eliza, seated primly at the table beside Roger, was already wearing the glazed
expression of near-fatal boredom. Well, who could
blame her? Half an hour later every face in the
room, save Oliver's, bore the same look.

"Bragg was at Murfreesboro with General Polk.

His left was at Triune and Eagleville with Hardee. His right, at Readyville with McCown." Oliver had just spent thirty minutes leading up to the Battle of Stone's River.

Delia and Roger sat in the back row, where they could easily see the heads in front of them nodding. The program almost always ran to Confederate cookery or architecture or fashions. When Oliver was invited to speak (and for some inexplicable reason that seemed to occur about twice a year) he regaled the members with battle strategy and casualty reports.

"Christmas Day saw a brief respite from the onslaught as the men observed various traditional entertainments. But the day after Christmas Rosecrans started out from Nashville, and the Confederate camps ended their festivities and prepared for battle."

"How much longer does this go on?" Roger whispered.

"Until the last Yankee swine croaks," Delia explained. "Or until Oliver loses his voice."

"The whole war didn't take this much time," Roger grumbled.

"You're thinking of the miniseries." Delia patted his leg, urging him to be patient. She planned to nap through the rest of the program.

"Not until the thirtieth did Rosecrans pull his full force together with McCook on the right, Thomas in the center, and Crittenden on the left. Bragg, meanwhile, had decided to meet Rosecrans on a line just outside Murfreesboro. The benefit to this was that his line covered all the major roads in the area.

"It is an interesting side note that on the evening

of the thirtieth, one band began to play 'Home
Sweet Home.' The melody was then taken up by
both sides as the battle-weary soldiers no doubt
thought of their own home sweet homes and the
loved ones they'd left behind.''

Delia was skeptical. If all those men were that
homesick, she thought, why didn't they just get up
and leave? That would have been an effective end
to the stupid war.

''. . . and Bragg mistook this maneuver for the
main thrust. He expected Rosecrans's troops to
mount an assault on his left flank.''

Roger's squirming was beginning to irritate
Delia. He didn't even enjoy listening to *her* anec-
dotes about the Old South. Whatever had inspired
him to accompany her tonight? Every single Son
and Daughter in the room had fallen into a lethar-
gic trance, induced no doubt by the droning of
Oliver's voice. Not to mention the overabundance
of detail he insisted on providing.

''The third day of the battle was actually two battles in one. The action was divided into two distinct
engagements separated by a full day of relative
calm. By the thirty-first, the Confederates were
celebrating a complete victory.

''Unfortunately Rosecrans believed (quite in error,
as it happened) that his troops were surrounded
by Confederate forces.''

Somewhere around the explanation for Rosecrans's delusions, Delia nodded off. She woke only
when the sound of chairs being pushed around
pierced her reverie. Looking up, she thought she
spotted relief on Eliza's face. And there was no
doubt about Roger.

''Before you go,'' Oliver said, bringing the whole

room to attention, "I have just one more item on the agenda. I'd like to declare my candidacy for president of the SDC." He stopped and flashed a televangelist smile at the crowd.

A few people applauded politely. Oliver nodded to acknowledge them, then turned to nod at Eliza. Eliza Wilson Leach seemed frozen to her chair, looking straight ahead at the room full of people who were pushing eagerly toward the door.

"Thank God that's over," Roger said, standing and stretching his long legs. "Can we escape now?"

"Don't you want to stay for the coffee and cookies?" Delia asked sweetly.

"I'll make coffee at my place. Now let's get the hell out of here before another battle begins." Roger took her arm and led her firmly away from the crowd that had gathered near the refreshment table.

Outside, the air whipped at them as they crossed the parking lot to Roger's sports car. Delia got in as quickly as she could. "Why don't you buy suitable transportation for a man your age?" she asked crossly.

"What? A wheelchair?" Roger started the engine and turned the heater to HI. It blew cold air most of the way to his apartment.

Roger's apartment had surprised Delia the first time she'd visited. It still did. He had a system of organization that would have baffled the greatest minds of the century. The front room, which others no doubt would have called the living room, contained two metal lawn chairs, an army desk, and wall-to-wall pine shelves held together with brackets and screws. The shelves held pristine boxes con-

taining an assortment of model cars. Roger organized, inventoried, and probably sang lullabies to
those boxes, but he never, never opened them. Once
Delia had found him grieving over a small patch of
mildew, and when she'd pointed out that only the
box was damaged, Roger had looked at her as if
she'd just killed his dog.

Aside from the models, however, there seemed to
be no rules for arrangement. The desk held piles of
what could only be called stuff. Papers, pictures,
takeout-food containers, and dirty clothes spilled
across the desktop. A framed print leaned against
one side.

"Make yourself comfortable," Roger said, sweep-
ing one arm in the general direction of a dilapi-
dated chair. "I'll get coffee."

"Wonderful," Delia muttered, knowing it would
take him several minutes to locate a coffeepot. She
gave one chair a gentle shake and decided to pass
it by. There were several large pillows scattered on
the floor, so she settled onto one of those, pulling
her coat around her for warmth.

"Did you pay your electric bill this month?" she
called.

"Probably," Roger answered above the noise of
running water. "I almost always do."

Delia wondered if she could persuade him that
they should continue the evening in his bedroom.
The bedroom, in contrast to the rest of the place,
was always immaculate. Probably because the only
thing in it was a bed. But at least that was always
made with hospital corners and clean sheets. Still,
Delia wondered why some of the junk from the
other rooms hadn't spilled over into that one as
well.

ALL THE CRAZY WINTERS

"It'll be ready in a minute," Roger said, reentering the room. He chose the same chair that Delia had earlier rejected, seemingly unaware of its delicate condition. "Are you cold?"

"I'm freezing," Delia told him. "Do you have heat?"

"Of course. It's on. You seem to be cold a lot these days. Sounds to me like thin blood. You probably need to eat more beef. Good hearty meals."

"Never mind. What did you think of the meeting? And don't say I didn't warn you."

"True, you told me it would be dull. You didn't say just *how* dull, but I'm willing to forgive you. Is Oliver always like that?"

"Yes. But he's more tolerable when he's not the guest speaker. In fact, tonight he was a last-minute choice."

"Why invite someone to discuss a subject that so clearly bores the entire membership?"

"Because, dear Roger, the SDC is thirty years old and we've had a meeting once a month for all those thirty years. We're fresh out of invigorating topics. Do you have any idea how many times we've heard about antebellum beauty hints? Or Old South Christmas customs?"

"I see. So every now and then you throw in a *really* dull evening. I wonder if there's some aspect of the Confederacy that I could cover for the Sons and Daughters. A Yankee perspective, perhaps?"

"Don't push your luck. You were only allowed in tonight as my guest. That's once in a lifetime. Guests are required to join—and your family fought on the wrong side of the war—*or* they get one freebie visit and they're never allowed through the door again."

"Why?"

"What do you mean why? That's the rule. Only true Southerners allowed. It's meant to make the rest of you aware that you don't fit in."

Roger arched one eyebrow. "Then perhaps I'll join the Historical Society." The Jesus Creek Historical Society was a fierce rival of the SDC, having been formed for just that purpose. Those who could not establish the proper documentation for membership in SDC were welcomed warmly into the other organization, which consisted largely of elderly widows who spent far more time researching eligible older gentlemen than digging into historical events.

"Don't you ever get tired of looking at the same old faces all the time?" Roger went on. "I mean, when's the last time you accepted a new member?"

"We get new members all the time. I believe that Eliza's daughter-in-law just joined."

"That's not new. That's just a branch of the same dynasty that's been there since time began."

"After all, Jesus Creek is a very settled community. We don't have unlimited new blood to inject into our cultural maintenance. Besides, it's nice to have continuity. There aren't many family traditions left."

"I see. This is like handing down Grandma's good silver to the next generation. I wonder if the young people have ever thought of starting their own traditions."

"Why should they? Don't you miss the old days sometimes? When you could walk the streets after dark without getting attacked? Or when families sat together after dinner reading or listening to the radio?"

"Or when people died of pneumonia? Hey, and how about that well water that we carried for miles just so we could soak in a good-sized washtub before crawling into a feather bed that sheltered God knows what kind of vermin and sneezing ourselves half to death? Now that was fun."

"Don't be difficult," Delia told him. She refused to admit that he had a point. Besides, he knew perfectly well what she was talking about. "I don't see any harm in a bunch of old friends getting together to remember the past."

"I don't either. When it's their *own* past they're resurrecting. We've talked about this before, though, Delia. They're trying to time-trip into another century. Have you ever taken a good look at Eliza, for instance? That woman is wearing her great-grandmother's dresses."

"Eliza is a conservative woman. Black is very becoming to her."

"How do you fit in with the rest of them? Vegetarianism must seem pretty radical to Eliza. And you do love your microwave, don't you?"

"That's because I *do* remember the past so well. I appreciate not having to slave over a wood cookstove all day, whipping up dinner for some pigheaded, pork-bellied cretin. Why can't I take the best of both centuries, Roger, and combine them? I'm very happy with things just the way I have them."

"Well, I suppose I should be grateful for that. With your love for tradition, there's not much chance you'll toss me aside for a grammar-school Romeo."

Delia rose and headed for the kitchen. "You may

convert me to your philosophy if you keep this up. Perhaps I'll start a new tradition."

In the kitchen she took both Roger's cups from the counter, rinsed them with tap water, and poured coffee. It wasn't that she didn't understand Roger's arguments about the SDC and her own interest in genealogy. For Delia both of them were hobbies, agreeable ways to pass the time. History amused her. Especially when she stopped to consider how soon *she'd* be history. And would some later generation look back and try to emulate this century?

She could imagine Roger's response to that idea! "Certainly," he'd say. "They'll all dress like twentieth-century matrons dressing like nineteenth-century belles. Talk about a confused world."

"What else shall we argue about?" she asked, returning to her nest of pillows.

Roger took the cup she offered and stretched out in his chair. "Your dalliance with the local constabulary during my absence?"

"Ah," Delia said. "Who spilled the beans?"

"Oliver told me as soon as we got to the meeting. Did Reb know anything new about Estelle's death? Did he figure out why she was roaming the neighborhood in her pajamas?"

"Nope. I wonder if anyone's asked Frankie Mae. Her back windows look right out over the library parking lot. She may have seen something."

"As I recall, Frankie Mae once saw Elvis working at a diner in Benton Harbor."

"Okay. I get your point. Maybe Walt Jr. would know something. He was spending the weekend with Estelle. Surely he'd have noticed she wasn't there."

"Has Reb asked him? I'd think that would have been the first step. After all, Walt is almost certainly the sole heir, therefore the most likely suspect."

"Reb's been checking into every conceivable motive. He's even gone so far as to get a list of everyone—I mean, everyone—who holds a library card. I'm sure he spoke with Walt as well," Delia said. "But I'd sure like to know what Walt said."

Roger nodded toward the telephone. "Why don't you call Reb right now? Get him out of bed. Then we can end this conversation and move on to something more . . . ah, personal."

"Because, my dear," Delia said simply, "I wouldn't know whose bed to roust him out of."

CHAPTER

11

ELOISE'S DINER DISPLAYED A PLAQUE OVER the milk shake machine reading EST. 1945. It was Delia's belief that the only change since opening day was the Tennessee Vols calendar by the cash register. The Formica counters and metal-frame chairs, the music on the jukebox, even the old black man who washed dishes made Delia think of handsome young soldiers and the Andrews sisters. She couldn't get enough of the place and always took out-of-town guests to Eloise's for the world-famous corn bread and the atmosphere.

Quite by accident Roger and Delia found Reb at Eloise's on Tuesday morning. He was working on a plate of ham, eggs, biscuits, gravy, and hash browns while Eloise struggled to keep up with his coffee consumption.

"Mind if we join you?" Roger asked, pulling out a chair for Delia.

Reb motioned with his fork and mumbled something that Delia took for invitation.

Delia settled herself at the table and tucked her purse between her feet. "Reb, Roger and I were thinking about Estelle's death last night. It's not that I'm implying anything, you understand, but I've heard that Walt Jr. was spending the weekend with his mother. Have you spoken to him? I mean, about why Estelle would have wandered over to the library at such an ungodly hour."

Reb nodded. "First thing I did. Walt said he left for home early Sunday morning. He said Estelle likes to sleep late on her days off, so he didn't bother her. Just left a note on the kitchen table."

"So she was still in the house on Saturday night when Walt went to bed?"

"Yep." Reb took time out to chew a bit of buttered biscuit. "And if you're wondering how reliable Walt is, the coroner agrees."

"I beg your pardon?"

"Estelle definitely died late Saturday night or very early Sunday morning as the result of a blow to the back of the skull with a heavy object, most likely a hammer. That's what the coroner says. I gave him a call and told him to hurry it up. He got back to me yesterday." Since Jesus Creek had no coroner, the few suspicious deaths that occurred in Reb's territory had to be investigated by a state coroner. Unfortunately, this system tended to produce a backlog, with small-town corpses getting lost at the end of the line. It could take as long as a month to receive a coroner's report.

"Stomach contents and that sort of thing," Reb went on. "Myself, I just don't know how a man can go digging around in other people's bellies. Not quite normal, if you ask me."

"Is it possible that the vandalism occurred either

before or after Estelle was killed?" Delia asked.
"I'm wondering if there might not be two different
people involved."

"Could be," Reb said. "That might explain why
the front of the library was untouched. If the burglar found Estelle's body, he probably decided to
leave right then."

"So how does this affect your investigation, Reb?
I suppose asking for alibis for the entire town would
be pointless."

"Always was. What sort of alibis do you think
people have for middle of the night? Everybody
claims to have been home, in bed. Besides, we don't
have suspect one to question."

"Wait a minute," Delia said. "Saturday night.
Oliver's house fire."

"Uh-huh," Reb said. "Forty million people milling around, getting in the way of the fire department. Are you suggesting that the fire was supposed
to divert us from the library?"

"Well?" Delia turned her coffee cup over to allow
the waitress to fill it. "It's possible, isn't it?"

"Yeah, but sort of pointless. No one would have
been paying attention to the library at that time of
night, anyway."

"Maybe the killer was just being cautious. You
know, in case a patrol car happened to wander by."

"Delia," Reb said, sighing. "Pointer Reeves
works the night shift."

Pointer was the only member of the Jesus Creek
police force who did work at night. He covered the
mean streets alone, as it were. Essentially though,
Pointer was known to have several hideaways in
which he could park the patrol car and sleep.

"You're right," Delia agreed. "It would definitely be a wasted effort to divert Pointer."

"Well, so much for that," she said to Roger, after Reb had finished his breakfast and left. "Apparently the fire was just a coincidence."

"Maybe not," Roger said, draining his cup for the third time. Anything labeled coffee was his idea of a nutritious breakfast. "How likely is it that a murder and arson would occur on the same night in Jesus Creek? How many murders do you have around here? How many cases of arson?"

"Not many," Delia replied. "It is odd, isn't it? Well, at least the coincidence makes for good gossip. I heard Walt Jr. is coming back to town this week to pack up Estelle's things. I'd like to talk to him. You don't think it would be insensitive of me, do you?"

"Yes. Insensitive of you to ignore me while playing amateur detective. Reb has matters firmly in hand. Don't get involved."

"I'm not involved. I just can't stand mysteries."

Reb raised one eyebrow, but Delia, devouring a bran muffin, didn't notice.

"Remind me to call Charlotte later," she said. "If I don't check in, she'll send out the rescue squad."

"Lucky you. Your daughter actually cares about you. Why do you always sound resentful about that?"

"Cares, hell. She thinks I'm an idiot who can't take care of myself. She gets more like her father every day."

"The heart of the problem. What did you think your children would be like when you chose the man to sire them?"

Delia sighed. "At the time it seemed like a swell idea."

"It always does. No doubt someday you'll think I sounded like a swell idea, too."

"Don't pout, Roger. You'll get no special treatment. I outgrew my need to comfort men years ago."

"Well, then, if that won't work, why don't we go back to your house and do something useful?" Roger grinned.

"Roger, I haven't even had my breakfast yet. It beats me how you can claim not to be a morning person and still think of sex before your eyes are fully open."

"I was talking about weather-stripping your doors," Roger said with wide-eyed innocence.

"Oh. I suppose we could do that, then." Delia finished the last of her muffin and checked her watch. "I've invited Sarah Elizabeth for lunch, so what say you go by the store and pick up what we need? Then you can drop by later. There's time first to go by Estelle's house and see if Walt's there. If he's not, we could leave a note asking him to phone."

Roger shrugged in defeat. "Yes, sure, fine. We'll interrogate Walt. Poor guy. He won't know what hit him. Maybe you can browbeat him into confessing to everything, including Jimmy Hoffa's disappearance. And then we'll get back to normal."

Sarah Elizabeth picked at her salad, shoving bits of lettuce and carrot around on the plate. "I'm so glad," she said, "that it's just veggies. I was afraid you'd have this huge bunch of food, and I know my willpower wouldn't have held up."

"You're dieting?" Delia said. "And here I've been

worried that you were going to starve because you didn't like my salad."

"Oh, no. It's delicious. But I guess I've eaten so much lettuce lately that I've lost my appetite for it. Or maybe my body just doesn't need as much food now. I've lost ten pounds already. Just ten more to go. And I'm awfully tired lately, too."

"That's from dieting," Delia assured her. "Have you considered the possibility that your body doesn't want to be thinner?"

Sarah Elizabeth shook her head. "No, I think it's lack of sleep. I haven't gotten used to the new house. And sometimes Lindsay James gets up at night to check on Mother Eliza. You know, to take her hot milk when she can't sleep. Every time he gets out of bed, it wakes me."

Delia eyed the young woman sitting across from her. There were dark circles under her eyes. "I don't think you need to lose any more weight," she said sternly. "You look a little thin as it is."

"Me? God, no. I'm healthy as a horse." Sarah Elizabeth shifted in her chair and speared a cauliflower bud with her fork. "I've been kind of tense lately, I guess. Probably from the diet. You know, not sleeping well because my stomach growls all night." She gave a high-pitched little giggle.

"I can't imagine why you'd want to diet if it makes you feel bad." Delia was firmly opposed to weight-loss programs of any sort, beyond the old-fashioned regime of eating sensibly and getting plenty of exercise.

"It's just that Eliza is so slim, you know? And she looks elegant in clothes. Things sort of hang on her, like a model." Sarah Elizabeth gave a wistful sigh and put down her fork.

"Eliza happens to be naturally thin. When we were in school, she was considered unattractively skinny. Which just goes to show how things have changed in the last twenty-five years."

Sarah Elizabeth attempted another bite, changed her mind, and placed her fork carefully on the plate. "I wish I were skinny. It sure would be easier to gain weight than to lose it."

"Well, if you insist on renouncing food, I hope you're at least getting regular checkups. You did have one before you started this diet, didn't you?"

Sarah Elizabeth shook her head. "Oh, no. But Eliza told me it didn't matter. She even wrote out a diet plan for me to follow. She's been really great. And she helps me pick out clothes, too. I never worried much about that until I met Lindsay James."

"Now that's something I'd like to hear more about. Where you're from, what you did before you were absorbed into the Leach family. What's your own family like?" Delia finished her own lunch and got up to pour them more coffee. She'd have liked to give Sarah Elizabeth a bracing cup of herbal tea, considering the case of jitters the girl had already developed from this pointless diet, but it might upset Eliza's planning.

"Oh, we're not anything like Lindsay James's family. My mom and dad both work. We're not rich, you know, or anything like that. I think they were both relieved when I got married and quit school because my younger brother starts this fall, and my folks really couldn't afford to send both of us, not even with my scholarship."

"You've got a scholarship? That's wonderful. What sort?"

Sarah Elizabeth gave Delia a dreamy little smile.

"Oh, it was for art. I'm not very good, though. I just mostly got lucky."

"You must have talent if you got a scholarship." Delia set the cup in front of Sarah Elizabeth, who shook her head at the offer of cream.

"No, not really. It was a fluke. But anyway, I don't mind not being in school. It's great living here, in that big house. And now that I've got this job at the library, well, things couldn't be much better, could they?"

"You like Jesus Creek, then? I'm glad. Sometimes when a young woman is newly married, adjusting not only to her husband but a mother-in-law like—that is, a mother-in-law—a new environment on top of it is more than she can bear."

"It's not really new," Sarah Elizabeth said. "My grandparents used to live here, ages ago. I was only about one or two years old, but I remember coming to visit them. My mother says I can't possibly remember, but when I first came here with Lindsay James, I went straight to their old house, and it was just the way I remembered it. Well, a little more run-down, but you know what I mean."

"Who were your grandparents? I'll bet I knew them. Let's see, it would have been not quite twenty years ago, is that right?"

"Oh, you wouldn't have known them. I asked Eliza and she had no idea who they were. They weren't the sort of people who'd have been hanging around with y'all."

Delia squinted across the table at her. "What sort of people would hang around with us?"

"I mean, my grandparents weren't well-to-do or . . . oh, you know. Like the SDC. Everybody who's anybody belongs to that. Well, my grandparents probably never even heard of it. They were too busy just trying to get by to worry about stuff like that."

"Sounds as if they were very sensible people, if you ask me. But they don't live here anymore?"

"No, they moved to Ohio years ago. My mother's sister got sick and my grandparents went to take care of her—for just a little while, they thought. But she died pretty soon after that, so Granny and Gramp stayed to take care of all her kids."

"Do you see them often now? Maybe they'll come back here to visit now that you're living here."

"I doubt it," Sarah Elizabeth said, and frowned. "They're pretty settled in up there, and I don't think either one of them especially cares about Jesus Creek. Like I said, they weren't anything special here. It was just a place where they lived."

"Had they lived here all their lives, then? Or just moved here for a few years?"

"Oh, I think they were both born here, but I'm not sure. I never asked."

"So your Confederate ancestor would be on your father's side, then. I mean, if you don't know the history of your mother's family."

Sarah Elizabeth glanced down at her folded hands for a moment. When she finally looked up, she whispered, "Will you keep a secret? I haven't the slightest idea about that. Eliza dug up all my family records. She tried to explain it to me, how I was related to somebody who'd fought in that war and all that, but I couldn't follow it. It's way too complicated for me, and besides, I don't really care about it."

"But you're a member of the SDC," Delia protested.

"I am. But only because Eliza *decided* I should

join. After she'd checked out my ancestors and all. I hated to tell her that it bores me. She went to a lot of trouble, after all, and I know it's important to her that I get into the club. Eliza says everyone in the family belongs to SDC. And it doesn't really matter, just go to a meeting now and then and maybe fix up some refreshments if you're on the committee." Sarah Elizabeth sounded breathless, as if she were defending herself against some accusation.

"I'm sure you'll develop an interest after you've been around us for a while," Delia said soothingly. "Or at least, maybe find a speciality that suits you. Literature of the period, maybe. You like reading."

Every member of the SDC had a special interest. For Delia, it was the mechanics of genealogy. On several occasions she'd spoken to the group about researching one's family tree. Oliver's special interest was also genealogy, but in SDC meetings he shone as the expert on detailed family histories. Estelle had taken custody of the subject of style—how things were properly done by proper ladies and gentlemen of the period. Roger had suggested to her one time that she give the group a lecture on how the ordinary people had lived. "Hand to mouth, scrounging for food, that sort of thing," he'd said. Estelle had only given him a puzzled glance and changed the subject.

"That might work," Sarah Elizabeth said, after a moment's consideration. "Eliza has been sort of pushing me to write a speech for one of the meetings. But I'm terrified of getting up in front of people and talking."

"I can fix that for you right now," Delia told her. "You don't speak to *people*. You get up there and look at me. Speak directly to me and to no one else. I can almost guarantee, you won't even notice the other people in the room."

"I don't know. . . ."

"Trust me. I used to teach fourth graders and I was responsible for coaching the annual Speakers of Importance. That's the same advice I always gave my students, and not one of them even came close to fainting away. Some of them even won awards in the regional speech contests."

Sarah Elizabeth giggled to herself. "If I fainted, I'll bet Estelle would pull smelling salts out of that purse of hers—oh, dear. I'm so sorry. I just keep forgetting that she's dead."

Delia nodded. Over the past few days she'd forgotten a few times herself. Once she'd gotten almost to the telephone, meaning to call Estelle about some trivial matter, before reality struck.

"Never mind," she said, reaching across the table to pat Sarah Elizabeth's hand. "Now I've got an idea. Let's check out this family of yours. Maybe I can help you understand how it works. Do you remember a name? Any name that Eliza might have mentioned."

Sarah Elizabeth thought for a minute while Delia waited. "My maiden name is Vickers, so I know she must have used that. Daddy was from Jesus Creek, too, so maybe it was his family that she checked on. Eliza seems to know more about me than I know myself."

"She probably had you thoroughly investigated before you married Lindsay James," Delia said. "No, no, I'm only kidding." For a minute there, Sarah Elizabeth had looked terrified. "Vickers is a great place to start. I'll get the book. You think about the rest of your family."

When Delia returned to the kitchen with Oliver's book, Sarah Elizabeth wore a triumphant smile. "Mom's maiden name was Holland," she said.

"Excellent. One of those families should be in here." Delia turned to the index.

"Is that Oliver's book?" Sarah Elizabeth asked. "Frankie Mae came in this morning asking about it. But I thought Pamela said all the copies had been burned."

Delia smiled. "I'll tell you a secret, but you have to promise not to breathe a word to Oliver. He had this printed up himself, you know. At Lindsay's print shop. Kay gave me this copy. She said it's common practice to print extras, in case of errors."

"Oh." Sarah Elizabeth smiled.

"Now, here's a Vickers," Delia said, "Page twelve. If this is your family, they'd have been original settlers. That counts for a lot, especially where Eliza is concerned." Delia flipped a few pages until she'd found the Vickers reference. "Here we go. 'Lucius Vickers arrived in the area sometime in the 1830s. He owned the first whiskey distillery.' Aha! I'll bet he was a popular man," Delia said.

"He was a bootlegger?" Sarah Elizabeth asked with awe. "I don't think that could be my family. Eliza wouldn't appreciate that at all."

"I don't think it was exactly frowned upon back then. Besides, Eliza wouldn't care as long as somewhere along the line your family fought for the Confederacy."

"If you say so," Sarah Elizabeth said doubtfully.

"After Lucius married, he had ten children. Haven't you ever wondered why these women didn't *kill* their husbands? I'd think it would have been worth the risk just to avoid bearing—and rearing—all those kids."

"Eliza says back then people were much more willing to make sacrifices for their country."

"Willing, or they just had no choice. Okay, it says that Lucius's son, Alonzo Vickers, was a corporal in the CSA. Doesn't say which regiment, but that's probably recorded in the back. Oliver put in an entire appendix devoted to veterans of the Civil War."

"Eliza always calls it the War Between States. You know, for the longest time I thought that was a whole new war that I'd never heard about in school."

Delia had to laugh. "How far north did you live, child? Didn't you ever read *Gone with the Wind?*"

"I saw the movie once, but I didn't like it. Scarlett was sort of brassy, I thought."

"Funny. I always considered her a brainless wimp. She kept screwing up her life and everybody else's. Well, anyway, I think this is almost certainly your family. Tell you what, if you like, I can dig up some more information for you. It'll give us an excuse to have lunch again."

"I'd love another lunch, but I really don't want to put you to a lot of trouble. Honestly, Delia, I don't want to know any more about this."

"Then how about if I help you make up a list of literature from the period. We could work together on your speech for the SDC if you like. That should put you in good with Eliza."

"That's so sweet of you! But do you promise not to make me listen to my family history? Promise?"

Delia raised her right hand. "I promise. Nor will

I inflict mine upon you, although, truth be told, it's far more impressive than the Leach family story."

"It would almost have to be!"

CHAPTER
12

DELIA WAS JUST PASSING PATE'S HARD-
ware store, having reached a comfortable walking
stride, when she heard the singing. " 'I've got joy,
joy, joy, joy down in my heart, down in my
heart. . . .' " It was Miss Constance Winter, no
doubt about that.

"Good morning, Miss Constance!" Delia called as
soon as she'd spotted the old woman. Today Miss
Constance had a curly brown wig perched like a
beret atop her own gray hair. To compliment this,
she was decked out in a red plaid scarf and peach-
colored raincoat. Delia hoped the coat was warmer
than it looked. The temperature had risen to an
almost comfortable twenty-eight degrees, and the
afternoon sky looked as if it were tuning up for
snow flurries, at the very least.

"Hello, my dear," Miss Constance answered back.
"See what I have here?" Miss Constance held out
an aluminum pie pan full of brownies and peanut-
butter cookies.

Delia stopped to look. While she did not consider herself a finicky sort, she cringed at the prospect. Miss Constance had been known to concoct recipes on the spur of the moment, throwing in this and that and Lord knew what else. She'd probably been pushing these goodies all day, with no takers. "Well, perhaps just one," Delia said, selecting a cookie and tucking it carefully into her own coat pocket. "Can't be too careful about our figures, can we?"

"We can't. Men aren't as easy to come by as they once were. No, ma'am. It's a joyous thing to be a beautiful girl. Was one myself, once."

"You're still a beautiful girl. The rest of us age, but you, you just get better and better."

Miss Constance tucked her head shyly into her shoulder. "You flatter me. Take another doodad." She thrust the pan into Delia's face, beaming broadly as she did so.

"Uh, just one more," Delia said, taking a brownie this time. "You're very thoughtful. It's been lovely chatting with you. Goodbye, Miss Constance."

"We must have you to dinner soon," said Miss Constance vaguely as Delia walked past.

As Delia continued her course (five times fast around the courthouse and half speed back home) she heard Miss Constance's singing begin again, fading gently in the November wind until it had died away in the distance.

"That crazy old woman's gonna die of frostbite." The speaker was a woman who'd just stepped out of the video store.

"I think she's immune," Delia said, keeping her pace. And it was probably true. Miss Constance had been walking the streets, day in and day out, for as

long as Delia could remember. She was, true to her
name, a constant, the one fixture to be counted on
in the small world of Jesus Creek. And before her
there'd been the other crazy Winters, unique every
one.

There were few people out, Tuesday afternoon
never having been a heavy day for shopping. If Estelle were alive, Delia thought, I could stop by the
library and have a cup of cocoa with her. If Eliza
wasn't such a bitch, I could stop by and have a cup
of coffee with her. Ah well, as Miss Constance would
probably say, there's always poo-poo in the water
where you want to swim. Which, as best Delia could
tell, meant that nothing's perfect.

With her options exhausted, Delia finished the
walk and resigned herself to making her own coffee
or cocoa or whatever seemed most likely when she
got home. She wondered if Walt Jr. had returned
to town yet. It would be difficult for him, she imagined, to sort through all Estelle's possessions by
himself. For one thing, the house was crammed top
to bottom with Estelle's possessions. For another,
Walt was a devoted son; he'd seemed strained at
the funeral, despite his effort to hold himself together. Maybe she'd call tonight, just to check on
him. She'd decide later whether she wanted to offer
assistance.

As Delia made her last orbit of the courthouse
and headed down Main Street she once again heard
Miss Constance's voice lifted in song. This time it
was "Jesus Christ, Superstar."

"You sure do spend a lot of time in my kitchen,"
she said.

Roger was waiting for her, with a pizza already

baking in the oven. "But not enough in your heart," he said.

"More than you know. Can you throw some coffee in the pot? I'm pooped. That cold air takes more out of me than the walking." Delia wiggled out of her coat and gloves and piled them on a kitchen chair. Then she collapsed into a chair herself and began removing her shoes.

"There are certain forms of indoor exercise that will not only burn calories and keep you in shape, but warm your soul as well."

"I just had this conversation with Miss Constance. She says we girls have to keep our figures because men are so hard to come by these days."

Roger nodded. "Good ones, at any rate. How was lunch? Did the newest Leach tell you anything?"

"Uh-huh. She hates genealogy."

"God!" Roger said, clearly stunned. "And you let her out of here alive? Or does the club plan to grab her up in a large bag and lock her in a dark room until she's been suitably brainwashed?"

"She's really quite personable," Delia said, pointedly ignoring his sarcasm. "It's funny, to me at least, that she's absolutely awed by Eliza and that whole family. Probably worships Lindsay James, too. I hope he's got sense enough to appreciate her."

"Well, maybe if Momma orders him to. How do you like your pizza? Well done or completely black?"

"Easy on the black, please." Delia leaned forward and propped her elbows on the table. "I think you'd like Sarah Elizabeth, too, if you'd take the time to meet her. She's very young and very shy, but there's a lot of potential there. She's bright, just hasn't been around long enough to recognize the fact."

"Here," Roger said, sliding a pizza slice from spatula to plate and setting it in front of her. "What caused you to recognize her genius? Did she give you the formula for nuclear weapons?"

"It's her eyes, smartass. She takes things in; she just doesn't know how to interpret them yet." Delia pulled a sliced olive off her pizza and popped it into her mouth. "I wonder how long it will take her to figure out the mess she's gotten herself into."

"You mean marrying a Leach? Maybe she likes it. Some people find great wealth is worth a few sacrifices."

"I don't think money is a big motivator for Sarah Elizabeth. On the other hand, she did say that her own family isn't well-off. They used to live here, by the way. Vickers. Ever heard of them?"

"Not me. But then, I travel in a small circle. Just you and a couple of drunks down at the mission."

"We don't have a mission."

"Well, it's high time we got one. Speaking of missions, mine is to conserve your energy. Finish your dinner and I'll let you help."

"Aren't you a sweet man?" Delia reached across for another slice of pizza. "Maybe there's some Southern gentleman in you after all."

"I keep telling you, I'm from Chattanooga. How much more Southern can I get?"

"And I keep telling you: you people were Yankees. Still, there's always hope of conversion."

"Eat your dinner. I'm a devout carpetbagger already. Don't you get just the least thrill from sleeping with a Yankee?"

"Sometimes," Delia said, and batted her lashes at him. "Sometimes."

Walt Jr. answered his mother's phone on the third ring.

"Delia, how nice of you to call," he said breathlessly. "I've been cooped up in the house all day. Almost didn't find your note on the door, and then I got involved and forgot to call you back. Maybe I'm being overly sensitive, but I'd rather expected that someone, some of Mother's friends, might drop by."

"Most likely they're not aware that you're back in town," Delia told him. "I wasn't sure myself. Just thought I'd give it a try."

"Well, I'm glad you called. This house is terribly quiet. You know, Mother was always sort of chattering and bustling around. I don't consider myself superstitious or anything like that, but I swear, Delia, it almost seems as if the house has died. It's empty. Do you know what I mean?"

"Yes," Delia said, "I do. Would you like me to come by tomorrow and give you a hand?"

"I'd love it if you'd come for a visit. I won't make you help. Mother was a pack rat. Do you know she's got a chest full of my school papers? And even half-used notebooks that must have been left from grade school."

"That sounds just like Estelle. No doubt, though, once you've sorted through it all, you'll find that she's also kept wonderful treasures—family heirlooms, photos of relatives and friends."

"But I can't help feeling like a vulture when I dig through her belongings. After all . . ."

"I understand. But Estelle certainly meant for

you to have them, in any case. No question there. I think she'd be thrilled that you appreciate them. The question is, do you have the room? I'd understood that you live in an apartment."

"I do. Which brings up something else. I'd like to discuss it with you when you drop by."

"Fine. How about if I get there around noon? I'll bring lunch."

"No need," Walt assured her. "Mother has the cupboards stocked. I'll look forward to it."

Roger was waiting for her when she ended the phone conversation. "Did I hear you say you're going over there with Walt? You think that's smart?"

"Why not? Surely you don't think it's going to ruin my reputation. After all, I'm already hanging around with you."

Roger pointed a screwdriver at her. "Don't get wise with an armed man. I was talking about the danger to your physical person. Walt may very well be the one who did in Estelle."

"Don't be ridiculous, Roger. I've known Walt since he was born."

"You know the trouble with you? You trust too much. You think Sarah Elizabeth is just precious. But you have to admit she married into a wealthy family. Maybe she's nothing more than a gold digger. You think Walt adored his mother. Maybe he adored the family silver."

"Do you want me to go around questioning the motives of everyone I know?"

"Yes, frankly. Listen, Dee, people want things. You have to figure out what they want before you can deal with them on a safe level."

"I agree that everyone wants something. I just don't think that everyone wants money. Look at you. You could have seduced Eliza. Instead, you swept me off my feet."

"Money isn't my thing, true. But do you know what is?"

"Ha," Delia said smugly.

"Here." Roger thrust a roll of strip insulation at her. "Hold this, and your tongue. You know I'm right, but you're too stubborn to admit it." He started with the living-room windows, checking locks to be sure they worked. "Look, Dee. These top windows inch down. Cold air comes in at the top. You have to lock—I repeat—lock them to keep warm." He demonstrated by flipping the lock a few times.

"I'll admit that people want things. I'll admit that very often they want money. But I know a lot of people who want other, more important things. And I know perfectly well how to lock windows. But some don't have locks."

"Such as?" Roger asked.

"Eliza. She's always had money. She doesn't particularly want to lose it, I'm sure. But her family honor is what she cherishes most. And family unity. When we were children, Eliza positively worshiped her father. I remember visiting her, and she would drop everything as soon as her daddy came through the door. Her whole world revolved around him."

"If you ask me, that's sick." Roger was struggling with the plastic cover that seemed permanently stuck to the insulation strip.

"It was. But I didn't realize that until after her father died. Eliza nearly had a nervous breakdown. Couldn't function for months. And by that time she was married and Lindsay James had already been born. Of course, from an adult perspective, I could see that her father had never appreciated her attention."

"Really?" Roger was half listening. He was carefully running the adhesive-backed strip along the edge of the window.

"You'd think that would have taught her a lesson, I know. I'd think it, anyway. But if you've noticed, Eliza treats Lindsay James the same way. Nothing he does seems to please her."

"I thought you said she was big on family."

"Yes, but by her own definition, family is a blood-related unit. She thinks it happens by divine decree. Eliza has never done anything to promote the unity, you understand. She just takes it for granted that Lindsay James, being her son, will respect and love her."

"We need another screw for this lock," said Roger. "That should take care of it."

"Here." Delia found a box of screws in Roger's toolbox. "Meanwhile, Lindsay James keeps on trying to impress his mother. It's pitiful to watch, I'll tell you. But now that he's married, and has Sarah Elizabeth to adore him, maybe he'll grow up."

"Why should he?" Roger asked. "You said Eliza didn't get over her daddy."

"Yes, but Eliza's husband didn't love her the way Sarah Elizabeth obviously loves Lindsay James. Franklin James always loved Estelle. Or at least, I thought so. You'll no doubt tell me I'm a romantic fool, but I think some great passions never dim."

"I see I've finally convinced you. Come over here and hold this in place for a minute."

"Of course," Delia said, holding the lock where Roger told her, "Walt Sr. thought Estelle hung the moon. And as far as I could tell, the feeling was mutual. Funny, isn't it? Because Estelle and Franklin James seemed destined to be together. Or maybe that's just an idea left over from my youth. Do you think it's possible that some of us never quite see things the way they really are?"

"No doubt. Estelle never did." Roger stood back to admire his work. The lock was firmly in place. He shot the bolt, drew it back, shot it again, and ran his hand around the top of the window. "No draft," he said triumphantly.

"I don't think I've ever needed insulation. This weather has to be a mistake. Obviously it was meant for Canada."

"But Delia, dear heart, things have changed."

Roger had convinced her to let him spend the night, claiming he needed to be there to detect drafts in order to prevent them. He spoke a convincing case. Delia left him watching the late news while she creamed her face (and added a little extra moisturizer around the eyes).

She'd have to invite Sarah Elizabeth to lunch again. A sweet young woman. Delia could imagine, though, what a screwball she'd be if Eliza got a good hold on her. Not, mind you, that Eliza wasn't a dear and valued friend. But Delia recognized her faults, perhaps better than anyone else. Eliza would grind Sarah Elizabeth into the same sort of dull-edged stone as Lindsay James. There was something about her personality, her need to control other people and force their affection, that made Eliza seem cruel. But she wasn't, Delia knew. Delia had seen her crying for her father, had seen the love she'd lavished on the senile, incontinent old man just before he'd died. Why, Eliza wouldn't even allow him to go to a nursing home, which was where he'd certainly needed to be. She'd fed and bathed him, changed his sheets a dozen times a day, and never, ever complained.

"Where's the blanket control?" Roger called from the bedroom.

"On the nightstand. Where else?" Delia ran a brush through her hair, checked her face in the mirror, and turned out the bathroom light.

If Eliza had tried so mightily to win her father's approval, why didn't she recognize that Lindsay James was doing the same thing now? Delia had seen the boy practically turning handstands, jumping like a nervous rabbit, even rearranging his life to make time for Eliza's petty wishes. And she'd watched Eliza dismiss him with a wave of her hand and some thoughtless comment about his inability to handle finances or fix a car's engine. Never a word about his superior management of *The Headlight*. Not a single hurrah when he was named valedictorian. No praise from Eliza for his levelheaded behavior throughout his teens, when most children were hell on wheels.

Of course, Franklin James had adored his only son. Maybe that was part of the problem. Lindsay James was so much like his father. If Eliza had, as Roger and Reb suspected, been jealous of her husband's feelings for Estelle, she might be transferring those feelings to her own son.

Delia stopped in the middle of the hall and shook her head. A few psychology classes and she was analyzing everyone in town. No doubt it was just that Eliza and Lindsay James spent so much time together. If Charlotte lived with Delia, they'd probably hate each other, too.

"I didn't think we'd need the electric blanket," she said, sliding in next to Roger.

"I'm an old man. You can't expect me to keep you warm all night long."

Delia moved closer to him and rested her head on his shoulder. "Eliza's really a decent person, deep down."

"I'm sure," Roger said. He nuzzled her neck and began to move his hand along her thigh.

Delia woke late the next morning. Roger was still curled up in bed. She eased her feet onto the floor and rolled, trying not to wake him.

The phone in the kitchen rang as she was making coffee. Delia tucked the receiver between her shoulder and right ear.

"You have to do something, Delia, and I mean this instant! Maybe, just maybe, that fool woman will listen to you, unless she has lost her senses completely and in that case—"

"Pamela? Is that you?"

"—she has to be removed anyway. Did you know about this, Delia?"

Delia shifted the receiver to her hand and sat down at the kitchen table. "I don't even know what you're talking about. Could you settle down and fill me in?"

Pamela took a deep breath before starting again. "I received an official notice from the board this morning. They thanked me politely for all my work since Estelle's death. And they feel sure, I'm quoting now, that I'll continue to be a valued and valuable employee under the new head librarian. The new head librarian, Delia, is Sarah Elizabeth."

Delia was literally speechless for a moment. "Pamela, surely someone's just made an error."

"That's what I thought, too," Pamela said, "so I called Eliza. She assured me that the notice is correct. In fact, she seemed to think I must be a real idiot for supposing that I would be appointed to the job. I ask you, Delia, am I not the only qualified person? Am I not the very person responsible for keeping this library running all these years? Well?"

"Of course you are," Delia said soothingly. "I certainly thought—Pamela, did Eliza give you any explanation? I mean, why would the board give Sarah Elizabeth the job when she's only been working there a week?"

"The board? The board does what Eliza tells them to do. That's why!"

Delia ran a hand through her hair and tried to think of something to explain this bizarre turn of events. "Why, Pamela? Eliza is surely aware—"

"Eliza hasn't been aware of anything in years. She told me that Sarah Elizabeth, as a member of an old and trusted family, would be more acceptable to the patrons. When I tried to point out that most of the patrons have never heard of Sarah Elizabeth, that bitch had the gall to tell me it was traditional for the head librarian to be a member of the original families. Have you ever heard anything so ridiculous?"

"No," Delia said, "I haven't. Eliza can't be serious. Why, Sarah Elizabeth doesn't even have her degree."

"Eliza has an answer for that, too. She claims Sarah Elizabeth will be working toward her degree beginning next semester. Which means, of course, that she'll need extra days off."

Delia was stunned. Surely Eliza and the board couldn't be serious about this.

"Well?" Pamela said. "When are you going to talk to her?"

"To Eliza? Pamela, I think you've overestimated my influence. I'm only a library volunteer. I have less power than you as far as the board is concerned."

"Forget the board," Pamela snapped. "It's Eliza you'll have to deal with."

"Either way—"

"You're part of the old families. Apparently that counts substantially."

Delia felt a headache coming on. She hadn't even had her morning coffee and here was Pamela screeching at her about something for which Delia was not responsible and could not change. "I'm sorry, Pamela. I don't think Eliza gives a damn what I think. Your best bet is to confront her yourself."

"Well, the least you could do—"

"My biscuits are burning," Delia said firmly. "I have to get off the phone."

In the bathroom she turned on the water, eager for a hot shower to ease the stiffness that had moved into her muscles during the night. It was either the cold weather or Roger. She wasn't sure which. Either way Delia supposed she'd learn to live with it.

It would probably be a good idea to call Eliza, she'd decided, and invite her to lunch. Couldn't have Eliza getting jealous of Delia's time with Sarah Elizabeth. That would make the situation worse for the poor unsuspecting daughter-in-law. And Eliza would probably react just that way. Delia would call her as soon as she'd dressed and had breakfast, but she absolutely would not say a word about Pamela and the board's decision.

Roger was on the phone when she emerged from the bathroom. He looked ridiculous, standing there in the middle of the kitchen stark naked. Delia stepped up behind him and wrapped her arms around his middle.

"Uh-huh," Roger said into the mouthpiece. "I'll certainly tell her, Frankie Mae. Yes, I'm sure she'll want to call you back. No problem. I'll tell her you said so." He hung up the phone with a sigh. "My God, that woman could drive a saint to drink."

"What did she want?" Delia asked, following him back into the bedroom.

Roger reached into the closet and took his robe off the hook. "Wanted you to know," he said, slipping one arm into a sleeve, "that Lindsay James Leach was attacked last night. In particular, she wanted you to know that *she* called to tell you. She seems to think it's important that she get the news out ahead of everyone else."

"What do you mean *attacked*? By whom?"

"That seems to be the question on everyone's mind. Frankie Mae says Reb has issued an APB. According to her, Lindsay James said there were two men but they slipped up behind him, so he didn't see their faces."

"Then how does he know there were two?"

Roger gave her a peck on the cheek. "Call Frankie Mae back and find out."

"Was Lindsay James badly hurt. Oh, my goodness. What about Eliza and Sarah Elizabeth? Are they all right?"

"Frankie Mae didn't say. Why wouldn't they be?"

"Well, if someone broke in . . ."

"Did I forget to mention that Lindsay James was at his office? Sorry. I'm barely awake and it was Frankie Mae, after all. You can't blame me for being confused myself."

"Was this last night? Why on earth was Lindsay in the office at night?" Delia stopped. "God, that sounds just like the questions I've been asking about Estelle, doesn't it?"

"Lindsay James was not, so far as I know, in baby-doll pajamas when he was attacked. And yes, Frankie Mae says he's fine. Just has a lump on his head."

"That's the strangest thing. Estelle in the middle of the night in the library, Lindsay James in the middle of the night at the paper office—"

"Sounds like you're playing Clue. I'd like to get a shower. Do you mind whipping up something for breakfast while I do that?" Roger took her in his arms and gazed deeply into her eyes. "Exercise makes me ravenous," he said.

"It's been hours since you got any exercise," she told him. "But I'll make breakfast anyway. Poor Lindsay James. Poor Sarah Elizabeth."

"I'm sure they have insurance. It can't be that bad."

"Insurance? Well, yes, of course they have insurance. But I was thinking of how frightened she must be by this."

"Oh, I thought you were concerned about how they'd rebuild. Loss of income, all that."

"Income? Roger, you're not coherent."

"I guess I forgot to mention the fire, too, huh? Well, I told you, it's early."

"Fire? Yes, you do seem to have omitted that. What fire?"

"*The Headlight*. After Lindsay James was bonked on the head, someone set fire to the office. Left him lying there in the middle of it. Fortunately he came to in time to get out. But I understand from Frankie Mae that the newspaper office is completely gone."

CHAPTER
13

WALT JR. SERVED COFFEE IN THE KITCHEN of his mother's home. "I apologize," he said, "for the offerings." He'd sliced a Sara Lee coffee cake for dessert and served it to Delia on Estelle's best china. "I'd intended to pick up something from the bakery. Then I realized Jesus Creek doesn't have a bakery. Forgot where I was, I guess."

"I like this cake," she said, and wondered what it must be like to live in a town with a bakery. "And the coffee. To tell you the truth, I was a little worried you'd want me to drink tea. Your mother always did. People seem to think there's something wrong with those of us who hate the stuff."

"You don't drink tea? Not even iced?" Walt joined her at the table in the breakfast nook.

Delia shook her head. "I love the smell of it. Just can't stand the taste. How are you getting along here?"

"Slow." He shook his head. "I've begged boxes from every store in town, and so far I haven't even finished packing up the living room. Of course, a lot of it I'm not going to have to handle. Pamela Satterfield has agreed to take all the books, with the exception of a few that I'd like to keep."

"Agreed? I'll bet she drooled."

Walt grinned and nodded. "She practically knocked me down, trying to get in here before I could weed them out. But I'm wary of that woman. She'd probably snatch the family Bible right out from under me."

"You already know her intimately, I see."

"Mother told me about Pamela. I'll bet she's thrilled to have the job. Head librarian ought to suit her."

"It would have, had the board not given the job to Lindsay James's new wife." Delia shook her head to indicate that she had no explanation for this.

"I'm surprised," Walt said mildly. "From what Mother's said, I just assumed . . ."

"Yes," Delia told him. "We'd all assumed. Especially Pamela. Although, in my opinion, she had every reason to expect that the job would be hers. Anyway, enough about Pamela. What's happening here?"

"I thought I'd donate Mother's clothes to the thrift store. That's still around, isn't it? I know they used to give their profits to charity."

Delia approved wholeheartedly of his plan. "Yes, still here and doing good work. I'll call Wanda—she's running the place now—and ask her to arrange a pickup, if you'd like."

"It would make my life easier. I still have so much to take care of. Loose ends. Funny, isn't it? Someone like Mother can just disappear. Before you know it, all her possessions will be gone as if she'd never been here." Walt looked around the room, as if he couldn't trust his eyes to tell him that Estelle was no longer there.

"I don't think it will be like that exactly. I know it's worse for you, but please remember: a lot of us loved her. None of her old friends will pass a day without thinking about her."

"Mother seemed sort of, oh, abstract. Vague. But she made an impression, didn't she?"

"Absolutely. Probably a few that you don't even know about."

"Tell me sometime, will you? Some of the things about her that I don't know."

"I'll do that. Maybe the next time you come to town, when you aren't pressed for time. You are coming back to town, aren't you?"

He pushed a piece of cake around on his plate. "In fact, I wanted to talk to you about that very thing. This house and what I'll do with it."

"If you're looking for a realtor, I can recommend—"

"No, no. I'd never sell it. Do you realize this house has belonged to Mother's family for, what, a hundred years? No, I was considering something that would remind everyone of Mother, just as you said, Delia. What do you think of the Estelle Williams Carhart Historical Museum?"

Delia was speechless. She pictured the transformation in one breathless second. The house would be shined and polished, furnished with the best of the furniture and antiques in it now. The county would surely be willing to provide funds for maintenance. If not, maybe the SDC . . .

"You don't like it?" Walt asked, clearly disappointed.

"I love it! Are you kidding? I was just mentally taking over the project. Sorry, Walt, but I tend to get carried away when the subject turns to history. Roger could tell you stories."

"I thought you taught math," he said.

"I did. That's why I love history."

"Oh." He seemed baffled but decided not to pursue it. "You have ideas then? About how it should be done? Because I thought you might like to move the genealogy section of the library over here, maybe have a room—hell, the whole house, if you like. All the records and deeds and whatever it is you do. You could be in charge of the operation. Provided you'd do it for free. I can't pay you for this."

"Walt!" Delia exclaimed. She felt a weepy spell coming on and dug into her purse for the ever-present tissue. "You'd let me do that? No wonder Estelle always said you were a perfect son. I'd adopt you myself, if I weren't afraid it would turn you into a howling lunatic."

"Well, I don't have the slightest idea how we go about doing this. There may be zoning regulations or fees or Lord knows what. But I think it's a perfect use for the old homestead. I certainly can't live here. And I don't want the place to sit and rot."

"Estelle would love this. Almost as much as I'm going to. No, don't worry about red tape. I'll cut through it. The important consideration is you have to tell me what you *don't* want me to do. Sometimes I have a tendency to take over—just sort of plow right through with my own ideas."

"I hope you will. History and genealogy were Mother's interests, not mine."

"More coffee, please," Delia said, giving herself

one last sniff. "I promise I'll stop crying. It's one of my quirks. They say it comes from being born near the water, although I never figured out what kind of water."

Walt refilled her cup, then set the coffeepot down on a trivet. Standing behind his chair, he looked carefully at Delia. "Mother was a weeper, too. Was she like that always? Or was it something that came about later?"

"I don't remember," Delia said. "I don't recall being a weeper myself until I was grown."

Walt settled back into his chair. "I ask because . . . well, I found some letters in Mother's wardrobe. She still used that, did you know? Instead of closets. All the other bedrooms have been remodeled and had closets added. But Mother kept hers exactly as it was when the house was built."

"There isn't much room in them for clothes," Delia said.

"That's why she kept a few dresses in the wardrobe and packed the rest of her clothes into every closet, drawer, and cupboard in the house. Anyway, I found these letters tied up with ribbon and tucked in her jewelry box. They were from Franklin James to Mother."

Delia pinched off a small section of cake, carefully avoiding Walt's gaze. "Uh-hmmm," she said.

"Oh, it's okay, Delia. I know about Mother and Franklin James. After Dad died, Mother and I became very close. Almost like best friends, really. She told me the story of how Eliza wound up with Franklin James. Mother said she was brokenhearted for months."

"That's true. I remember spending most of the summer trying to console her. I honestly thought she might, well, do something silly. She was impulsive, God knows."

Walt laughed a little, sadly. "Impulsive. I suppose so. If it weren't for that, if she hadn't gone dashing out to the library that night, she'd still be alive, wouldn't she?"

"Is that what she did? Dash out?"

"I'm guessing," he said. "I think I remember hearing her move around that night. But Mother often did, you know. She had trouble sleeping sometimes and she'd putter around the house. Once she went out on the porch swing, and I found her sound asleep there the next morning."

"But you'd have heard the door if she'd gone out, right?"

Walt shook his head. "Not necessarily. In fact, I'm sure I didn't or I'd have checked the swing again. I just remember hearing her in the hallway outside the bedrooms. And then I guess I went back to sleep. The next morning . . . I was leaving before six . . . I didn't want to bother her. I knew if she'd had a bad night, she'd need the sleep. So I left as quietly as I could. God, if I'd stayed another day, at least I would have known. We'd have found her sooner." Walt rubbed one hand across his face and rose from the chair.

"It's terrible for you, I know." Delia sat silently to allow him time to recover. Walt was a kind man, gentle as his mother had been, but sensible, like his father.

After a moment Walt picked up his coffee cup and rinsed it in the sink. "I heard that the newspaper office burned last night," he said firmly.

"I passed there on my way over," Delia told him. "The inside is gutted. Poor Lindsay James will be lost. I hear he's got a lump on his head, but otherwise he's fine."

"That's lucky," Walt said vacantly. "I'm glad he's going to be okay. Lindsay James is a good guy, basically. I don't know how he got that way. Or maybe I've just inherited Mother's prejudice. Eliza Leach is one woman I can't stand."

"Unfortunately she's one of my lifelong friends. Despite her character flaws, I like her. But not always. Maybe I mean I love her, not like her. There's a big difference."

"Yes," Walt said. He returned to his seat. "Those letters were love letters, Delia. I'm talking about love, you understand. Not sex. Franklin James was still in love with Mother. I don't know if he'd said anything to her before, but the first letter was written about six months after Dad died."

"How odd that Estelle never mentioned it to me. She usually told me everything."

"Oh, you know Mother. Couldn't keep a secret if her life depended on it. But someone else's life depended on this. In the letters, he told her that he was tied to his family, that he didn't regret having married Eliza. And he went on and on about Lindsay James. But he just wanted Mother to know that he loved her and was there for her. He wanted to be her friend."

"I wonder if Eliza ever knew about this," Delia mused. "She's a possessive woman. I doubt she'd have wanted them to speak pleasantly, much less be friends."

"According to Mother, Eliza was always afraid that this sort of thing would happen. Mother said that Eliza knew from the very beginning that her hold on Franklin James was tenuous. I'll bet Eliza held a celebration the day Mother and Dad got married."

"Come to think of it, Eliza offered to pay for the wedding." Delia smiled to herself. "Estelle should have taken her up on it."

"Do you remember if Mother cried the day she married Dad? Some brides do."

Delia looked at him closely and tried to summon images from the distant past. "Walt, I know that Estelle adored your father. By the time she married him she was completely over Franklin James and knew just how fortunate she was to have Walt."

He reached across the table and took her hand. "You're a nice woman. I'm glad Mother had a friend like you."

"I was lucky to know her. You've no idea how much pleasure I'll get, for the rest of my life, just remembering her."

Reb had roped off the area around the newspaper office, but aside from a few pedestrians who slowed to look, no one was paying much attention. Delia stepped across the rope and walked to the doorway of the office, where Reb was talking to Lindsay James.

"I'm glad you're not badly hurt," she said.

Lindsay James turned to look at her, his eyes not quite focused. A patch of hair on the back of his head had been shaved and covered with a gauze bandage. "Yes. Thank you. My head hurts, but that's supposed to get better soon."

"Lindsay James is more upset than he realizes," Reb said accusingly. "He ought to be home in bed. That's what I've been trying to tell him all morning."

"Reb's right," Delia said. "Why don't you go on home, Lindsay James? Eliza is probably worried about you. And I'm sure Sarah Elizabeth is a wreck."

"I can't," Lindsay James said stubbornly. "Reb won't listen to me. This is important. Someone is doing this, all of this."

Delia looked questioningly at Reb, who shrugged and shook his head.

"First Oliver's house, then Estelle, now this," Lindsay James explained. "I've tried to tell you—"

"Look, if you'll go home and let me look around here, I'll see what I can come up with," Reb promised. "But you can't keep wandering around. The fire chief says this place isn't safe."

Lindsay James nodded and looked mournfully at the shell of his office building. "I'll have to get started on it right away," he said softly. "Rebuild it. Our family has always gotten the paper out on time. This will be the first deadline we've ever missed."

Reb took Lindsay James by the arm and tried to steer him out to the sidewalk. "Look," he said. "I'll walk you home. Just to make sure you get there."

Lindsay James shook his head. "There's no need, Reb. I'll be fine. To tell you the truth, I'd like some time to myself."

"Sure, I know what you mean," Reb said, but he kept a cautious eye on Lindsay James as the young man walked away from them.

"He could be right," Delia said, after Lindsay James was out of earshot. "All these things that have happened lately surely aren't coincidence."

"I tend to believe you're right," Reb said. He pulled a pack of Marlboros from his shirt pocket and tapped one out into his hand. Lighting it, he blew a neat circle of smoke that drifted up for a few inches before being caught by an air draft and carried away, a warped cloud of smoke completely unlike the ring it had been just moments before. "Lindsay James says he thinks there were two people in here last night. But he didn't get a look at either one of them."

"Two? Then maybe one of them set the fire at Oliver's on Saturday night while the other was at the library?"

"Could be. Or it could be that Lindsay James just imagined it. Maybe the fire started and he got excited and hit his head trying to get out."

"On the back? That doesn't make much sense, Reb, and it doesn't explain this sudden rash of crime. How long has it been since Jesus Creek has had murders and attempted murders and arsons and—"

"Yep." Reb leaned against the signpost that read MAIN STREET. "Yep, you're right. You were always the bright one, Dee. And the honest one. Even when nobody else'd tell the truth, there you were, charging in like a knight in armor."

"What on earth does that mean?" Delia was surprised, and oddly shaken, by this strange revelation.

"Something unusual is happening around here. Even the wind feels different lately. Oh, I noticed, but I was pretty sure that it would all get back to normal. You know, it didn't seem like anything I really had to deal with. Guess I was wrong."

"The wind feels different because there's a front coming in," Delia said. She'd never heard Reb talk like this before and it alarmed her now. "As for the other, I suppose we've been lucky to avoid it till

now. Small towns used to be safe from this nasti-
ness but not any longer. Do you have any idea what
to do about it?"

"Start from the beginning," Reb said. "Only this
time, I'll pay attention." Reb tossed his cigarette
onto the sidewalk and stamped it out with his boot.
"Come on. I'll walk you home."

"Good," Delia said. "I'd like the company. I just
came from Estelle's. Walt Jr.'s now, I guess. He's
decided what to do with the house."

But Reb didn't really seem to be listening to her.
Delia had the idea that he was watching the clouds
rolling in from the west, studying them, looking for
something she couldn't fathom.

Roger had decided that they needed a night on
the town. He'd insisted on a good restaurant across
the river in Benton Harbor, where they'd be anonymous and uninhibited.

"All set?" he asked. Roger was wearing a suit
and tie, something else he didn't usually do.

"I think so. My panty hose feel twisted, but I suppose that's normal."

Roger whistled when he saw her. "God, I love it
when you dress up. Do you have a garter belt? A
black one maybe. And fishnet stockings."

"You didn't say you wanted me to stand on street
corners."

"If you have a garter belt and fishnet stockings,
we won't even leave the house." Roger pulled her
to him and began to kiss her neck slowly and suggestively.

"You'll get a mouthful of foundation any minute
now," Delia warned him, but it was too late.

"Argh!" Roger pulled back and tried to wipe his

tongue on a handkerchief. "How can anything that
makes you look so good taste like that?"

"Because it's made with indecent chemicals.
That's how. Just as well. We need to hit the trail if
we're going to save our reservation. Those expen-
sive roadside diners get real uppity." Delia picked
up her purse and held the door for him.

"Whose idea was this anyway?" Roger asked ir-
ritably as he headed out the door.

"Yours, as I recall. If I know you, and I do, you
probably thought you'd convince me to spend the
night in some sleazy downtown motel."

"The thought had crossed my mind." Roger held
the car door open for her, then walked around to
the driver's side and got in. "But then I thought,
no, no sense in paying hard-earned money for a
cheap room when we could just run back here."

"Sensible even in the throes of passion. That's
my guy."

Roger's car had been running for several minutes, but the ongoing blast of cold air that hit Delia
let her know that the heater wasn't going to coop-
erate tonight. She was trying to convince Roger to
trade up when they saw the blue lights of a patrol
car parked in the circle drive of Twin Elms Inn.

"Oliver!" Delia said, and pointed.

Roger slowed to look, then said, "No. Reb. I'm
almost certain of it. See the profile?"

"No, no," Delia told him. "Pull in there. I mean,
something's happened to Oliver."

"How do you know?" Roger pulled the car into
the drive and stopped just a few feet behind Reb's
patrol car.

"It's just the sinking feeling in my stomach,"

Delia explained. "And because so much has happened lately."

Delia and Roger got out of the car just as Reb concluded his radio conversation with the police dispatcher. "Delia, Rog," he said. His expression said more.

"Oliver?" Delia asked.

Reb nodded. "Dead. Probably sometime last night."

"Like Lindsay James," Delia said. "Two attacks in the same night."

"How do you know Oliver didn't just drop from a heart attack or something?" Roger asked.

"Because," Delia explained, "there are too many other things going on." She looked to Reb for confirmation.

"She's right," Reb said, remembering his earlier conversation with her. "Someone beat Oliver to death with the standard blunt instrument. He was the only guest and he turned in early last night. Patrick was off at some meeting or the other, so no one saw or heard anything." Patrick McCullough owned the inn, but there was no live-in staff. It wasn't unusual for the inn to go for weeks at a time without guests.

"Which do you think happened first?" Delia asked. "The fire at the newspaper or this?"

"Don't know. Probably doesn't matter. There's an ambulance on the way. I'll have Oliver's body sent directly to the coroner and I'll raise hell to get the autopsy performed right away." Reb turned away from them and looked up at the stately columned house behind. "This old place survived the war and everything that's happened since. Do you reckon it'll survive what's coming next?"

"What's that?" Delia demanded. "Reb, you haven't started having visions or been thinking about joining some New Age cult, have you?"

Reb turned to face her and grinned wryly. "A new age. That's what it seems like to me, Delia."

CHAPTER
14

THEY SETTLED FOR ELOISE'S DINER. BY THE time the paramedics had loaded Oliver's body and Roger had been able to drag Delia away from the inn, he'd lost all interest in fine food.

"Probably my last chance," Delia said mournfully. "And I'm overdressed, too." She looked around her at the other diners, most of whom were wearing jeans and work shirts, or at most, denim skirts and sneakers. Kay Martin from the *Headlight* office was dining with a man Delia didn't recognize, and neither of them seemed to notice Delia.

"You stand out from the crowd," Roger admitted. He'd removed his jacket and draped it across a chair, then tucked his tie into the pocket and loosened his collar. "But you always do."

"Thank you, I suppose," Delia said, and sighed. "I'm starting to feel like a jinx. First Estelle, now Oliver. Not to mention the fires and whatever's about to happen next."

"Why do you assume something else will happen?" Roger asked warily. "You haven't got inside information or anything?"

"We seem to be on a roll. This is a crime wave, don't you think? But I have the feeling nothing is resolved. I doubt very much it's some maniacal killer. That leaves a killer with a single-minded purpose, and since the purpose hasn't been made clear, I think there's going to be more trouble."

"Only if you go looking for it," Roger warned. "Here. Take a menu and order." He handed her one of the menus that had been tucked in beside the napkin holder at their table. "I don't see how you can relate all these things anyway. Oliver and Estelle had nothing in common."

"Yes, they did," Delia insisted. "They both belonged to SDC, for one thing. They're both involved in family research. Oliver gave Estelle the first copy of—oh, damn."

"What? Don't just swear and leave me hanging."

"That book of Oliver's. First the library was broken into and Estelle was killed. We never found the book he'd donated. Oliver's house was burned and the fire started in the study where he kept all his copies of the book. And the only other place those books might have been was in the newspaper office. Kay told me they had extras, not to mention the plates for printing the new ones."

Roger leaned back in his chair to think about it. "Okay," he said at last. "Someone's killing because of a book. That's ridiculous, but I'll let you have it. If, indeed, all the copies of that book are now destroyed, then the trouble is over with. Reb may not have caught the killer, but at least we don't have to worry about any more deaths."

Delia shook her head stubbornly. "Not all the copies. I still have one," she whispered.

"Oh, hell," Roger said grimly. "I'd forgotten about that. Where is it?"

"At home, of course. Do you think I'd carry that boring book around with me?"

Delia closed her eyes and tried to remember if she'd mentioned the book to anyone. "Sarah Elizabeth," she said. "She's the only person who knows I have it. Wait, there'd be Kay. And she may have mentioned it to Lindsay James, but I'm not certain. It may be against the rules for her to give those things away. Who else have I mentioned it to?"

"My advice is to take that book down to the courthouse square first thing in the morning and burn it publicly. That's the only way you'll be sure the word will get around. If, and I'm not convinced, but *if* the book is what started all this, then you'd better get rid of it now."

Delia nodded. "I just got a chill down my spine. You don't suppose I could be in danger? No, that's silly."

"Why is it silly?"

"Because it is. Who's going to hurt me?"

"Probably the very words spoken by your friend Estelle when she marched out of the safety of her house and into the clutches of her murderer."

"Thank you for making me feel safe," Delia said tartly. "What's your problem?"

"I thought if I terrified you, you'd let me stick around to protect you."

"You'd give up the Grand Nationals of slot-car racing for me?" Delia asked skeptically. Roger's face showed strain. He was obviously struggling with the decision. Delia decided to let him off the

hook. After all, he needed a clear head to concentrate on the race tomorrow night.

"How about if we order dinner? Quickly. I've got
this burning desire to run home and make sure the
book is still there."

"Even better if it's not. Look, if someone really
wants that book badly enough to kill, then let him
or her take it while you're not home. What's in it
anyway?"

"Just history. You know, a lot of stuff about who
the original settlers were and where they came
from. Their descendants and what they did."

"That's all?" Roger asked doubtfully. "There
must be more to it than that."

"Not as far as I can tell. It looks to me like Oliver
just compiled a lot of well-known facts and published them. There are about three sections in the
back, things like veteran-pension lists and war records."

"Sounds like something a person would kill to
avoid reading."

"Precisely. Except for those of us who keep these
records, and that's half the population of Jesus
Creek. Consequently, no one could possibly care
what's in Oliver's book."

"You see? I told you it had to be something else.
Assuming that the deaths of Estelle and Oliver are
related. It could be just random." Roger tried to
look relaxed and cheerful but failed pitifully.

"All of a sudden you expect me to believe we're
having a rash of murders. And that they're simply
coincidence?"

"It happens. Stages, vibrations, harmonic con-
vergences, whatever. Please order your dinner."

Roger nodded at Eloise, who'd been standing by their table for a full minute, pen poised in the air.

"Eloise, I'm sorry," Delia said. "Just give me the vegetable plate and coffee." She tucked the menu back into its holder and waited for Roger to order his usual steak and fries.

Eloise sighed as she wrote the order. "You need a steak." She returned to the order window, shaking her head at Delia's choice.

"I'm trying to think of anything else they might have had in common," Delia told him. "Estelle, Oliver, and Lindsay James. After all, he was injured and certainly could have died in that fire if he hadn't regained consciousness when he did."

"Does his wife collect insurance if he dies?" Roger asked.

"Sarah Elizabeth? Don't be ridiculous. She's crazy about the boy. Besides, I'm sure Eliza has seen to it that Sarah Elizabeth won't collect a penny under any circumstances."

"Maybe Sarah Elizabeth isn't as innocent as you think. People have been fooled before."

"Not me. I'm an excellent judge of character," Delia said confidently.

"What was that you were telling me the other day? You must have been out of your mind to marry . . . ?"

"That hardly counts. I'd as soon suspect Eliza of trying to kill Lindsay James. Sarah Elizabeth is off the list."

Roger sat up straighter in his chair. "You know what? Could be that if someone really wanted Lindsay James dead, he's still in danger."

"Are you taking me seriously then? About there being a string of murders?"

"I always take you seriously. Whatever made you think I didn't?"

"But you've been arguing with me all night about this."

"Just trying to keep you alert," Roger said. "What do you think? Reckon Lindsay James ought to ask for police protection?"

"He'd probably be better off having his mother stick by his side. Maybe the object of the fire was to destroy the newspaper files and equipment. Lindsay James wouldn't ordinarily have been there that late, would he?"

"Beats me." Roger shrugged. "But why would someone want to burn down *The Headlight*?"

"To stop the paper being printed?" Delia suggested. "Or to stop something else being printed. Maybe we should ask Lindsay James what projects they've been working on."

"Maybe you should let Reb ask. Stay out of this, Delia. It's none of your business."

"I realize that. Well, in a way it is. All these people are my friends, you know."

"Everyone in town is your friend, but you don't clean their houses."

Delia frowned. "What does that mean?"

"It means I think you're getting carried away. Just because you watch *Magnum* doesn't mean you're a P.I. You don't know what's going on or how much danger might be involved."

"I wish you'd decide what you think. Either there's a serial killer loose in Jesus Creek or there's not. If there's not, fine. But if I can help find out who killed Estelle, why shouldn't I do it? I'm not a complete idiot, you know. I'm not going to stake out suspicious characters or get involved in high-speed chases—"

"Considering the condition of your car, I doubt you could."

"—but there's no reason why I shouldn't check out any ideas that occur to me."

"Just remember that I get the first *I told you so.*" Roger leaned back and flashed her a superior smile.

Delia might have thrown her glass of water in his face had Eloise not arrived just then with their order.

The next day Delia was awake early. Outside, the weather had gone from bad to worse. In addition to the bone-chilling wind that had started the day before, there was now a bitter November drizzle mixed with snow (what some weather casters insisted on calling *snain*).

Delia warmed a pan of milk for hot cocoa. Then she wrapped a heavy coat around her nightgown before going out to fill the bird feeder by the kitchen window. If the current weather was any indication of what the coming winter would be, Delia's birds would eat her out of house and home.

The cocoa was a welcome relief from the temperature and dampness outside. Delia settled in at the table and propped her feet on a kitchen chair. After the cocoa had thawed her bones, she'd fix a quick breakfast and then call Eliza. It might not be wise to tell Eliza what she thought about Lindsay James being in danger. Goodness knew, Eliza was a competent woman, but she could go off the deep end at times. Delia suspected that any mention of her son's being the target of a killer might do it.

And there was Sarah Elizabeth to consider, too.

She might be competent, and Delia suspected that she was, but she was very young and very much in love with Lindsay James. So how to bring up the subject without frightening either woman?

Maybe Delia could start by asking how difficult it would be to rebuild the *Headlight* office. That might give her a lead-in to ask what sort of work they did there, other than putting out the alleged newspaper.

What on earth could they do? she wondered. Printing, selling office supplies. If *The Headlight* had printed Oliver's book, might they be printing books for the other people? They might, she concluded, but it wasn't very damn likely. Jesus Creek wasn't big enough for more than one aspiring author.

It seemed logical to Delia (although she was sure Roger would disagree) that Oliver's book was the link. Suppose someone wanted to prevent publication of a family disgrace.

Delia hurried into the living room, where she kept a pile of odds and ends for future reference. The book was on her desk. Somewhere. She was fairly certain.

The History of the Original Families of Jesus Creek was tucked under the latest *TV Guide* and three saucers that had contained Delia's snacks for the last few nights. It might be a good day to stay home and clean, she thought, then decided that other concerns were more pressing.

Book in hand, she returned to the kitchen and grabbed a banana from the fruit bowl on the counter. She'd have to read it, *really* read it, and see if it contained any revelations with bearing on the recent tragedies.

Delia sighed and began again with the first page. Mineral deposits. The reasons settlers chose to stop here on the journey west instead of continuing to the Mississippi River.

By page four she'd found the first bit of halfway interesting information, nothing new but at least not as dull as geology.

Hiram Wicken, leader of a group of religious fundamentalists, led his commune into the hills of Middle Tennessee in the early-nineteenth century. Wicken, founder of the Blessed Way Commune, had acquired power over his flock by reporting to them the visions he'd received from God. The group indulged in neither alcohol nor certain foods, such as carrots and sweet potatoes, in the belief that orange and red fruits or vegetables were colored by the blood of saints. They did, however, eat grapes, purple being considered the color of heaven and therefore acceptable.

When the group first arrived in the area, the settlement was known as East Hill Town. Wicken's group took advantage of the nearby creek to hold a mass baptism immediately upon their arrival. This action caused the older residents to refer jokingly to the creek, as well as the community, as Jesus Creek. The name was adopted formally with the establishment of the post office in town.

Delia didn't think Hiram Wicken could have any connection to the present trouble in Jesus Creek, although those zealots sometimes surprised you. Oliver had included a partial list of the original

settlers, the ones who'd followed Wicken into the
territory. There were Wilsons and Leaches and
Hosts among them. Delia supposed that the few who
were listed only as *a family of seven* would be those
whose family lines had either died out or left Jesus
Creek altogether.

She skimmed pages, hoping something out of the
ordinary would catch her eye. If it didn't, she'd be
forced to read the entire book, and she'd read Oliver's prose before. Not a pleasant prospect.

"Aha," she said aloud. The Battle of Stone's
River, Oliver's subject at the last SDC meeting, had
only two paragraphs in the book, but something
ticked her memory. Wasn't it one of Eliza's ancestors who'd died there?

Delia checked the index for Leaches and Wilsons
and found the name she remembered. "Mary, the
feminist," she muttered. "Ran the farm alone,
didn't she?"

A math teacher should have spotted it right
away, she realized. Or any little old lady from the
community. Mary's child, and Eliza's direct ancestor, had been born more than ten months after the
Battle of Stone's River. More than ten months after
the death of the man who was supposed to be the
father.

Delia leaned back in her chair, amazed at the
implications. If this were accurate, if the dates had
not been printed incorrectly by either Oliver or Kay
during typesetting, then Eliza Wilson Leach was
not who she claimed. No sirree, Eliza Wilson Leach
was Eliza-Who-Knew-What?

Would the Leaches have allowed the marriage,
knowing this? Would Eliza be kicked out of the SDC

or could she produce some other illustrious family hero who'd served in the war?

"Stay tuned," Delia said cheerily.

Eliza was standing at the window, apparently waiting for Delia to arrive. She wasn't dressed for company, that much was clear. In a sweatshirt and old jeans, she looked more like Frankie Mae than the town's leading citizen.

"Sorry to track in the snow," Delia said, shaking her umbrella on the front steps. "I thought the rain had let up. Just about the time I got halfway here, it turned to snow."

"You can leave your shoes by the door," Eliza said absently. "We'll have coffee. Doesn't look like I'll be able to get back to the gardening for a while, anyway."

"Gardening?" Delia asked. She slipped off the soggy loafers she'd been wearing, noting that her socks were damp as well. She hoped that Eliza wouldn't notice her wet tracks on the carpet.

"I've been putting in mums for the tea. I'm having a few of the Women's Guild members over day after tomorrow for a planning session."

"But . . . mums? In November? During a cold spell? Eliza, they'll be dead in no time."

"What's important is that they'll look good for the tea. I can't have all those people arriving and seeing the front yard in its present condition, now can I?"

"Well, no," Delia said, "I guess not. But the snow may not let up before the tea. In fact, Bill Hall on channel four mentioned that we may be in for some sleet before the week is over."

Eliza pressed her lips together, obviously displeased with that news flash. "I'll have to think of something else, just in case. Maybe if I bought baskets of mums and set them out there just before the girls arrive . . ." Her voice trailed off as she led Delia into the dining room.

"We could have our coffee in the kitchen, Eliza," Delia said. "No sense messing up in here."

Eliza looked at her as if the words made no sense. "It's no trouble," she said. "Just have a seat and I'll be right back." ⸱

Delia took a chair and settled her purse on the floor. Eliza's dining room was magazine perfect. The wallpaper was an almost exact copy of the original, as were the curtains over the two tall windows. The table and china cabinet *were* original, passed down through who-knew-how-many generations of Wilsons or Leaches (the two families tended to blend together in Delia's mind). There was a fireplace on one wall, decorated with silver candlesticks and silver-framed photos of various family members.

Delia squinted, trying to identify some of the people in the pictures. There was an eight-by-ten color photo of Lindsay James and Sarah Elizabeth's wedding. All the others were black-and-white, or sepia, and showed dozens of stern-faced, straight-backed ancestors. One man Delia recognized. She'd seen the same pose in Oliver's book. Lindsay Zedediah Wilson and his three ugly daughters huddled together around a stand on which was displayed the family Bible. Delia thought it was an ironic setup, since she knew perfectly well that Lindsay Zedediah Wilson had been a drunk and a womanizer.

Above the fireplace there hung a carefully restored portrait of the young John Wilson, who'd died at Stone's River. Delia had seen it before and had always thought that Lindsay James was the spitting image of his ancestor. Well, knowing what she knew, this was clearly a case of seeing what she expected to see. Now that she really looked, young John didn't look a speck like Lindsay.

"Sorry to take so long," Eliza said. She was back and carrying a silver platter loaded with cookies, tarts, and sliced cake. "I'll just bring in the coffee and we'll be set." She placed the goodies on the table in front of Delia. "Would you mind terribly just helping yourself with the china and silver?"

Delia picked up the dessert plate as Eliza disappeared into the kitchen again. It really was china. One thing you could say for Eliza, she'd never trashed the environment with paper plates and Styrofoam cups and plastic forks.

Delia should have been used to it by now, this habit of Eliza's—always making a production of the simplest little thing. Of course, Eliza had very little else to do, if you came right down to it. No job. No small children—not that she'd been any less diligent about entertaining when Lindsay James was a toddler. And Delia supposed she ought to appreciate the time Eliza put into entertaining her friends.

"Sugar or cream?" Eliza asked when she returned with the coffee.

"No, just coffee," Delia said. She'd been drinking her coffee black for over twenty years, yet Eliza always asked.

"I wonder if it might not be warming up," Eliza said, peering out the window before she settled into a chair.

"I don't think so," Delia told her. "If I were you, I'd forget about the flowers. If the other members of the Women's Guild think they're supposed to bloom during a late-November cold spell, you should set them straight."

"I'm not surprised you feel that way," Eliza said.

Delia didn't want to take the time to analyze that retort. Eliza's zingers had long ago ceased to bother her. "How's Lindsay James?" she asked. "I saw him for a few minutes yesterday and he seemed a little foggy."

"He's fine. Stubborn, as was his father, you'll recall."

Delia couldn't think of a single example of stubbornness in Franklin James, but she had to admit that she wasn't trying very hard. "He seemed upset about this week's edition of *The Headlight*. He said this would be the first time it had ever failed to go to press."

"That's probably true," Eliza said. She was still looking out the window with a wistful expression on her face.

"That seems to me like a pretty good record. The Leaches have been printing the news for, what, two hundred years almost?"

Eliza nodded. "About that. I really don't know much about the paper, Delia. Franklin James and his father took care of it and then along came Lindsay James, so I never had to familiarize myself with the day-to-day operations. It seems to me that now would be a perfect time for Lindsay James to do something important with his life. He's young, just getting started really. You know, he has a degree in business. I insisted on it. Lindsay James actually intended to be a journalist, but I finally convinced him that any idiot could write little stories for the paper. A business degree, on the other hand, guarantees his future."

"I don't think any idiot can be a journalist, Eliza. In fact, it takes a particularly intelligent person to do it well."

"Why?" Eliza asked.

"Well, because . . . oh, for goodness' sake. For all sorts of reasons. And it seems to me that Lindsay James really enjoys it. I don't think I've ever heard him talk about anything other than running the paper."

"Lindsay James is devoted to his family, and I know you appreciate that as much as I do. So few children care." Eliza looked sharply at Delia, obviously implying that Delia's own daughter was less than admirable. "He took over for his father at the paper, but now that the whole place is cinder, Lindsay James can get on with his life."

"You don't think he'll want to rebuild?"

"He has no reason to. He's fulfilled his obligation. I told him that this morning."

"Well, Eliza, there has to be a newspaper somewhere in the town."

"Not really. I'm sure the editor of the *Benton Harbor News* will be happy to print our few items of interest—in return for Jesus Creek advertising. This town isn't big enough to require a weekly newspaper."

"But there's always been a paper here and it's always been printed by the Leach family."

"A few months ago I'd have agreed that you have a valid point. However, Delia, things just aren't the same around here anymore. The old order, the standards, they've melted away. If you're going to be somebody, you have to find new ways of doing it. The family name doesn't stand for much anymore."

Delia decided that was as good a cue as any. "I've been thinking about that myself," she said cautiously. "Reading Oliver's book has reminded me how many of the older families, the ones who practically ran the town a few years ago, are gone now. I suppose they felt the same as you."

"I suppose. And now with Estelle dead and that peculiar son of hers the last of the Carharts"—Eliza shook her head—"and Oliver, of course. There never was much hope for the Carhart line, as far as I could see. But Estelle didn't seem to notice."

Delia was not about to remind Eliza that Estelle's original plan had been to marry a Leach. Instead she said, "The Wilsons have always been able to weather the storms, though. I was especially impressed with one of your ancestors—Mary, was it?—who carried on and maintained the family land and holdings even after her husband died in the war."

"Yes," Eliza said. "I'm familiar with the story, Delia. After all, I've been researching the family for years, in addition to having access to all the research done by my father. Actually, there've been quite a few women in this family who have held things together. My mother, of course, wasn't one of them, but luckily I take after Father's side of the family."

"Maybe you get it from Mary. It must have been hell for her, being so young when her husband died. And then there was a baby to cope with. Of course, in those days, women had a particularly hard time of it, anyway."

"I doubt it was any harder for them than for us.

You know, I do think the snow is letting up. I don't mean to rush you, Delia, but I want to get these mums in place as soon as I can. It wouldn't do for them to look like they've been planted just for the tea."

"But they will have been planted for just that reason," Delia pointed out. "And every member of the Women's Guild drives past your house at least three times a week. Surely they'll notice."

"Well, of course they will. But still, I don't want them to *look* newly planted."

Of course, Delia reminded herself. It was appearances that concerned Eliza. "Well, don't let me keep you. I'm heading home to curl up by the fireplace anyway. The last thing I need is to catch a cold from walking around in the rain. Roger would never let me hear the end of it."

"Is he still around?" Eliza asked as she gathered the cups and saucers onto a tray. "Where did you say he came from?"

"Chattanooga," Delia said. "And he seems to be here to stay. He likes Jesus Creek."

"That's just what I was telling you earlier," Eliza said. "Things here are changing. The town just isn't what it was."

CHAPTER
15

"I DON'T KNOW," DELIA SAID. "ELIZA DIDN'T seem particularly disturbed about it. I'm sure she knew what I was hinting at." She was curled up on the sofa, her feet tucked under her and a cup of hot cocoa on the table to her left.

Roger was trying valiantly to build a fire in the fireplace. It was obvious to Delia that though he may have been raised a country boy, he'd forgotten all he knew of stacking kindling. She, however, was not going to be the one to tell him how to do it. Roger might be a reasonable man most of the time, but try to give him a little aid and instruction and he turned mule stubborn.

"Maybe she's just a cool operator," he suggested. The tiny flame that had taken hold seemed in imminent danger of dying, so Roger began to fan it gently with his hands.

"Could be. I'll bet she's already had the same conversation with Oliver. Sarah Elizabeth mentioned that they were talking about family research and Eliza seemed upset. Of course, Sarah Elizabeth wasn't paying attention."

"Uhm-hmm," Roger said. He added a few pages of crumpled newspaper and watched it flare. The fire was looking more promising by the minute.

"But if Oliver knew about Eliza's dubious pedigree, why didn't he just make the story public?"

"Maybe he wanted to intimidate Eliza."

"He's a braver man than I," Delia said sincerely. "To start with, I can't imagine how anyone would go about intimidating Eliza, and I can't imagine why anyone would try."

"Oliver was like that," Roger said, adding a few more twigs to the fire. "He enjoyed getting under your skin."

"True," Delia nodded. "I wonder if he actually did confront Eliza. I wonder, too, why no one ever noticed the discrepancy before."

"Because no one outside the Wilson family would have cared enough to notice. You're always on the lookout for names belonging to your family. If you happen to find something about one of Eliza's ancestors, do you make a note of it and tell her?"

"Heck, no. In the first place, genealogy around this town is almost a competition. I'm not giving any help to my main rival. And besides, I'd figure she already knows it. If I have access to a document, she's almost always been there before me."

"Exactly. No telling how many people have seen the same information, but from either lack of interest or time or whatever, no one ever stopped to figure up the time involved. Personally, I think you should make an effort to find out who the father of that kid was. That could be quite lucrative, if Eliza is embarrassed enough."

"I presume you're talking about blackmail, which I don't really have a problem with. But blackmailing Eliza is more than I want to deal with. She'd probably just conk me over the head with a fireplace poker and . . ." Delia's voice trailed off as the idea occurred to her. "You did say—"

It was obvious that Roger was thinking the same thing. He'd dropped the small log from his hand and it rolled quietly across the carpeted floor.

"I must have been joking," Roger insisted. "I certainly never thought Eliza killed Oliver."

"I think you were talking about Estelle. About Eliza wanting to be president of SDC?"

"That was definitely a joke. Who'd kill to be president of a club full of batty old people?"

Delia cleared her throat as a warning. "You're right, though," she said. "It is silly. That's not a motive. Is it?"

"On the other hand, you remember that couple in Nashville last summer? He killed her during an argument over an ice-cream cone."

"Yes, but those people were clearly deranged."

"Almost anyone who commits murder is," Roger said. "And if Eliza Leach doesn't qualify, then who does?"

"Well, if Eliza did kill anyone, and I'm not saying she did, then she ought to have run her course. All of Oliver's books are gone. Even the plates Lindsay James would have needed to print another batch."

"Except for the one you have. The one you told Eliza all about."

"Oh," Delia said. "That one."

"I can't believe I'm suggesting this, but I think we ought to call Reb."

"I am not about to call Reb and tell him I suspect Eliza Wilson is running amok and dispatching her best friends to that great soiree in the sky."

"Why not? It seems like a good idea to me."

"Well, because I'm not convinced she is. And I certainly wouldn't make an accusation like that until I have some sort of proof."

"What do you want? An obituary?" Roger poked at the fire, putting out the meager flame he'd managed to start.

"Look, I'll talk to Eliza."

"Wonderful. Tell her you know all about her nocturnal activities. Tell her you're going to report her to the police just as soon as you have proof that she's a crazed killer. That oughta loosen her tongue."

"This whole business has gotten out of hand. Just listen to us. For goodness' sake. Eliza didn't kill anybody. I'll just ask her, straight out, if Oliver was threatening to release the information about Mary. Eliza will tell me the truth and I'll promise never to let it pass my lips and that will be the end of it. If it comes right down to the wire, I'll even ask if she has an alibi for the nights that Estelle and Oliver were killed. I'm sure she will. After all, Sarah Elizabeth and Lindsay James live with her."

"Oh, right. Like they're going to tell you their mother was missing all night and came home with blood on her clothes. I think you're living a sheltered life. People commit murder. All the time. And you know what the friends and neighbors of the killer always, but always, say? 'She seemed like such a sweet little lady, just taking care of her forty-eight tabby cats and baking cookies for the neigh-

borhood kids. Who'da thunk she'd buried all those
bodies in the peony bed?' "

"You really are warped, Roger." Delia picked up
her cup and finished the last of her cocoa. "She
wouldn't hurt Lindsay James."

"Seriously, Delia," Roger said. He was satisfied
with the fire and joined her on the sofa. "What if
Eliza is killing people? Maybe she doesn't even have
a reason. Maybe it's not the book or her ancestors
or anything we've talked about. It could be that
Eliza is just crazy."

"Well, if it isn't the book or her family, there's
no reason to suspect her, is there? Anyone could be
nuts. For all I know, it's you. Lord knows you've
done some peculiar things."

"All in the name of love," Roger said. He took
one of her hands and pressed it to his lips. "I may
be mad with passion but—"

"There you go. Crime of passion."

"—only when I'm near you. Or when I think of
you. Or when I—"

"I've got the picture, Roger. And I feel the same
way about you. Now, have we finished this nonsense about turning Eliza over to the FBI?"

Roger sighed, resigned to his opponent's victory.
"I suppose. But if the subject comes up next time
you're talking to Reb, will you at least point him
in her direction?"

"I'll consider it."

"Look, why don't you come with me tonight?"
Roger said suddenly. "Cheer me on to victory."

"No way," Delia said firmly. "Fighting traffic in
Nashville is bad enough. And watching you race
makes me a nervous wreck. Besides, the weather is

rotten. Thank you, but I'd rather take my chances with a deranged killer."

It wasn't that she believed Eliza might be a murderer. Once Delia had spent a few private moments thinking about it, she realized how impossible it would be for Eliza to kill anyone. No, that wasn't her style at all. She'd just bully someone else into doing it for her.

But Oliver's book seemed to leer at her as she went through the living room turning off lights. "If you know something I don't," she told it sternly, "the time has come to confess." She picked up the book and studied it for a moment, then decided to carry it with her to bed. She could read through it again, and maybe her subconscious mind would give her a hint during the night.

With three pillows behind her and the bedside lamp on, Delia read again about the Hiram Wicken convoy, the formation of the town's first militia, and dozens of marriages and the resulting offspring. It was so obvious now that Mary Wilson had conceived her child months after her husband's death at Stone's River.

Delia wondered again who the father of that child was. From what less glamorous line was Eliza Wilson Leach descended? And why on earth wasn't good old Mary thrown into a tar pot when it was discovered that she was pregnant? Granted, medical science in those days was not advanced, but any old granny should have known the child was long, long overdue.

"Overdue children," Delia muttered, rubbing her eyes. She closed the book, placed it on the bedside table, and snapped off the light. "Overdue children, overdue books. Who pays the fine?"

The dream may have started then—Delia was never sure—but those words rang through it and were still clanging around in her head later when she woke.

Eliza, Mary, and Delia. The three of them were huddled around the handmade cradle of a newborn child.

"Long overdue," Mary said, pointing to her son.

"Shhh," Eliza warned. "Don't tell the whole world about it."

Delia didn't understand. Why would Eliza care? After all, it was obvious to anyone who looked that the child was overdue. Why, he barely fit into the cradle, even with his arms and legs wrapped around him that way.

As Delia looked down at the child she noticed for the first time that he was more than large. He was a fully grown man, dressed in a Confederate officer's uniform and laid out as if for his funeral.

As the three women stood there only Delia seemed to be puzzled. "What on earth are you going to do with him?" she asked.

"Why, he's just fine," Mary told her. "Just fine. Fine and dandy."

"Fine?" Delia asked.

Mary bent over and began to rock the cradle, gently at first, then harder and harder until the wood floor beneath it began to squeak in protest.

"Careful," Eliza said. "Be careful. That's dangerous."

"Nonsense," Mary told her. "The book said it's fine."

"What book?" Delia wanted to know.

"The library book. It's fine but it's overdue and there's no one to pay. Estelle is dead, you know. A fine thing. Fines are due and overdue and there's no one to pay because she's dead."

"But little Zithius is fine."

Squeak, squeak. The cradle rocked.

Delia woke suddenly, her breath coming in short gasps, her face burning from the adrenaline that coursed through her body. She couldn't have been asleep long. That was the first thought she had when her eyes suddenly popped open for no apparent reason and she saw that it was still dark. Must be bad prose before bedtime, she told herself, and rolled over onto her side. Watch what you read before retiring.

Then she heard it again. The squeaking she'd attributed to the dream cradle. Only this time she was certainly not dreaming.

It occurred to Delia that the squeak was coming from the living room and getting closer to her. She could hear her heart pounding in her ears. For an instant she was paralyzed, completely unable to move but aware of every sound and sensation. Trembling, she reached under her pillow and pulled out the kitchen knife she kept there. The next time Roger tried to give her a gun, she'd accept.

Don't let it be anything, she thought desperately. If she slid very quietly out of bed and stood behind the door ... Why on earth hadn't she taken that gun?

Delia moved on tiptoe across the room, trying not to bump into anything in the darkness. You were supposed to grow accustomed to that, she remembered. Maybe if she just stood perfectly still and stared straight ahead ... But blood was rushing so

furiously through her body now that it had affected
her eyesight. It was akin to tunnel vision, she
thought. Or what happens when you're dreaming
and about to wake up. The vision starts to go.
Maybe that was it. She was still in the middle of a
nightmare.

She heard footsteps moving closer to the bedroom
door. Were they her own? No. She was standing
perfectly still behind the open door, one hand on
the doorknob, the other clutching the knife. Definitely someone coming her way. Everything's coming my way, she thought. Everything's coming up
roses. Good God! She was losing it.

Even though she'd been expecting it, when the
man moved past the doorway and directly in front
of her, she gasped. He must have heard her because
he turned sharply, searching the darkness—or
maybe just disoriented.

What was it you were supposed to say when confronted by an intruder? Go away and I won't call
the police. That was it.

"If you go away now," Delia said firmly, "I won't
hurt you."

The intruder jumped, clearly as startled as Delia
had been by the words. His head twitched as he
tried to find an exit. The window was locked and
Delia, with knife in hand, stood too close to the door
for his comfort.

It came to her in a flash that she had the advantage. She was armed. The burglar, as far as she
could tell, was not. With the knife gripped firmly
in her hand, Delia reached behind her and flipped
on the overhead light.

"My God!" she said.

Lindsay James had put a hand to his face,

whether to hide his identity or to shield his eyes from the light, Delia wasn't sure.

"Lindsay James?" she said in disbelief. "What the hell are you doing?"

Lindsay James dropped his arm and let it hang limply by his side. "I know this looks odd," he said.

"You're damn right it does," Delia snapped. She kept the knife pointed at him, knowing full well that she wasn't going to use it. Not on Lindsay James, for God's sake.

"If you'll just let me explain," he said weakly. "Could we go into the other room and sit down? I'll explain and you'll see then that it's not what it looks like."

"It had better not be," Delia said, but she took two steps to the side, allowing him room to pass through the door.

Lindsay James went quickly into the living room and sat cautiously on the edge of a chair. Delia followed him, feeling guilty about holding a weapon on him, but still reluctant to put it down. She sat down at the end of the sofa, as far away from Lindsay James as she could manage.

"Now, what are you doing rambling around in my house at this hour?" she asked. She wasn't even sure what the hour was.

Lindsay James avoided eye contact. That worried Delia. "Sarah Elizabeth said that you have one of Oliver's books." He glanced up quickly and saw her nod. "I thought they were all gone, you see. When the office burned, I made sure I had them all in the pile."

"*You* set fire to *The Headlight*?" Delia asked. Now, that surprised her. She'd have bet anything

that Lindsay James would give his life to protect
the newspaper.

Lindsay James nodded gently. "I thought if I did
that, and made it appear that someone had attacked me, no one would stop to wonder about why
the fire was started."

"Good reasoning," Delia said. "Up until now no
one had. I suppose the problem is that you don't
want anyone to read the book and start asking
questions about John Wilson."

"You know?" Lindsay James asked.

"Well, certainly. I've been a genealogist for a
hundred years. Ten-month-long pregnancies sort of
stand out."

"Oh." Lindsay James seemed truly disappointed.
"I didn't anticipate anyone reading the appendix so
carefully. I should have known better, though, after
living with Mother all these years. As hard as I
tried, I never could retain all that information. It
just slipped out of my head as soon as I'd read it."

What was he babbling about? Delia wondered.
The appendix? Who on earth, outside of scholars
and confirmed masochists, would read an appendix?

"Mother was disappointed. She'd try to talk to
me about it, you know, about some ancestor or
other? And I couldn't remember which one she
meant, or what that one had done or even what
century we were talking about."

"Lindsay James, I appreciate your frustration.
Just as a side note here, may I suggest that you
share this with your wife? She's feeling guilty about
her inability to develop a passion for genealogy."

"Is she?" It didn't seem to interest Lindsay
James.

"Please get back to the book and why you broke into my house to steal it. You must realize the information in Oliver's book is available to anyone who takes a little time to look it up in other documents."

"Of course it is. But Mother said no one had ever bothered before, and if we just kept quiet, no one ever would. Then along came Oliver. He's always been a spiteful bastard. Mother says it's because his own family line is so questionable."

"Really?" Delia said sarcastically.

"At any rate, Mother was upset when Oliver started implying that he would let the whole town in on it. Mother would have been laughed out of SDC, no doubt about that. Those people don't care about anything real. They're so caught up in history that they can't take the time to show compassion for living people."

"I'm sure your mother could have proved her Confederate background some other way, Lindsay James. There must have been plenty of her ancestors who served in the war."

"Sure, but John was the only officer. Mother has been waiting years for her chance to become president of SDC."

"Well, a Confederate soldier is a Confederate soldier, after all. Isn't one just as good as another? Besides, Eliza has the appointment all sewn up."

"Oh, they say that. Every member of that club believes it, I guess, but has there ever been a president descended from a piddling foot soldier? Hell, no. They've always been the children and grandchildren of officers. And then Oliver decided to run for president. He did it just for spite, you know. No,

Delia, Mother would have been destroyed if she'd lost that chance."

"And you thought getting rid of Oliver's books would protect your mother? Lindsay James, whatever happened to that logical mind of yours?"

"Well, when I thought only Oliver knew, it seemed simple enough. But you've figured it out. Oh, my God! You haven't told anyone, have you?"

Delia wondered which was the proper response. Should she tell him no one else knew, so that he'd go quietly home and stop acting like a third-rate burglar? Or should she tell him the truth and introduce him to the real world?

"Yes," she said. "I've mentioned it to a few people. No one seemed to care."

Lindsay James looked up and met her eyes. Delia couldn't guess what the expression on his face meant. It was either resignation or relief.

"How many?" he asked quietly.

"Heavens, I don't know. Lindsay James, it doesn't make any difference. No one is going to say a word to Eliza because every one of us has some skeleton in the closet."

"Delia, this is a little more than having a horse thief for an ancestor. The entire family history is at stake."

"Now look," Delia said, leaning forward. "I've had just about enough of this crap. Roger is absolutely right. We're all lunatics. These people, these ancestors that we all babble about like they're living next door, they don't even exist. They're just names on paper. We wouldn't recognize them if they knocked on the door right now, and what's more, we probably wouldn't like them much, either. It's very likely that the father of Mary's child was an upright, law-abiding, God-fearing man."

"Well, of course he was," Lindsay James said. "But the SDC wouldn't see it like that. They'd just say, 'Oh, well. He was a deserter. We can't have that, can we?' "

"I beg your pardon?" Delia said. "Who was a deserter?"

"John Wilson. I mean, that's the word they'll use, isn't it? Mother said so, and she despaired just thinking about it."

"John Wilson deserted? You mean, he just went back home and . . . he's the father of Zithius?"

"Sure." Lindsay James frowned. "What did you think he did?"

"I thought he died at Stone's River."

Lindsay James smiled. "You thought he died? In battle? Is that what you've told all those people?"

"Sure it is. How would I know he was a deserter?"

"In the appendix," Lindsay James explained. "The pension roll for Confederate veterans? He's not there."

Delia was stunned to silence. "I don't believe this," she said finally. "You've broken into my home, burned your own business, just so no one could read the stupid appendix?"

"Well, you see, don't you, what it would have done to Mother to have that come out?"

"If Oliver had even noticed, and I doubt very much he had, how were you going to stop him from telling?"

Lindsay James looked surprised. "Why, just the way I did. I killed him."

CHAPTER
16

"LET ME GET THIS STRAIGHT," DELIA SAID, leaning forward on the seat. "You killed . . . actually murdered . . . two people just so the rest of us wouldn't find out that some ancestor of yours was a deserter?"

Lindsay James nodded somberly and reached inside his bulky field jacket. "You see, Mother has always taken care of me. You know how she is. Always safeguarding her family. Well, when I realized what Oliver had in mind, I thought, just this once, I'll do something for her." He held the hammer loosely in his right hand, as if he'd just taken a break from building the barn to chat.

"Does Eliza know what you've done?" Delia asked cautiously. She held the knife firmly, but her hand had started to sweat. She could imagine all the possibilities—dropping the knife, Lindsay James throwing the hammer and hitting her before she had a chance to use her own weapon. Use her own . . . weapon? Stick a knife in Lindsay James? The thought made her queasy.

"Not yet," Lindsay James admitted. "I was going to tell her after the last time. You know, after I got rid of Oliver for good. But then Sarah Elizabeth mentioned that you had one of the books. I thought maybe I could sneak in here and get it. But I should have known you'd be a light sleeper. Mother is, too."

"Go back to the beginning," Delia said. "Tell me how this all started. Surely you didn't burn Oliver's house and—"

Lindsay James nodded enthusiastically. "You see, I thought that would get rid of the books. He'd just picked them up the day before. I didn't think he'd sold any. He was planning to have a party, autograph the books. I'd forgotten about the one at the library, though. Oliver had mentioned it at dinner, but I was so busy . . . after I set the fire at Oliver's house, I had to run over to the library."

"I see," Delia said. She was trying to keep him talking until she could come up with a no-fail escape plan. Lindsay James blocked her exit by the front door. The only chance was to dash across the living room and into the bedroom. If she could shut that door and lock it, then call for help, she'd be okay.

"Boy, did I have a hard time with that!" Lindsay James chuckled. "That library office was such a mess. I didn't think I'd ever find the book, but I finally did. And then Estelle came toddling in. She took one look at me, and do you know what the old bat said? 'Why, Lindsay James, I declare.' "

Delia eased closer to the edge of the sofa, hoping to get a good start when she made her move. "And you couldn't think of any way to explain your presence?"

"Right," Lindsay James agreed. "There wasn't much to say. So I hit her, of course, but you probably already know that."

"Um, yes. And then you went on home?"

"Exactly. Mother was awake when I got there, and I even considered telling her then, but she just wanted warm milk. You know, sometimes I do that for her at night when she can't sleep. And I didn't feel it would be a proper time to explain—not when she was trying to sleep and all."

"Very thoughtful," Delia said.

"Then I saw that Oliver wasn't going to leave it alone. I had planned to tell him that we'd lost the plates, so we couldn't print any more copies of his book, but he still had one. He said we could use it to reset the book."

"And that's when you decided to kill him."

"Someone would have done it sooner or later anyway. But by that time I realized that I might never be rid of that book. So I just burned the whole shebang, office and all. Now all that's left is to get rid of the copy you have."

Delia took a deep breath. Maybe this would work out after all. "Oh, is that all you want? Well, why didn't you say so? I'll get it for you. It's on the nightstand in the bedroom." She rose slowly and started for the bedroom, mentally calculating the time it would take to slam the door and barricade herself in the bedroom. "Don't go away now," she called over her shoulder. "I'll be right back."

It took more effort to walk slowly than it would have to run, but Delia knew that every moment was crucial now. Just a few steps, grab the door, shield herself . . .

She'd just stepped inside the bedroom, was about to reach for the door with her free hand when she felt Lindsay James behind her. Delia turned, one arm—the one with the knife—raised to protect herself. Lindsay James swung the hammer. It grazed the side of her head, but the brunt of the blow was deflected by her arm. Or rather, by the knife.

She'd nicked him, but the knife couldn't have done much damage through the layers of heavy clothes he wore.

"Damn it, Delia, don't make this hard."

"Are you nuts?" Delia shouted back at him. She stepped behind the door, hoping to push it against him. There was no way now she could keep him out of the room, but at least she could put something solid between herself and that hammer.

"Of course I'm not nuts. I'm trying to take care of my mother. I've always tried to do that. What's wrong with a son being good to his mother?" Lindsay James grabbed the door with one hand and ripped it out of Delia's grasp.

Trapped, Delia looked frantically around for a way to escape. In less than a second she realized that there was nowhere to go. The blow Lindsay James had given her earlier wasn't serious, or at least she didn't think it was, but there was blood running down her face. His arm was raised again, above her head, and she could see the hammer moving toward her in slow motion. This is it, she thought, and brought the knife up, burying it in Lindsay James's shoulder.

* * *

Delia had not been bothered by visitors. Neither the doctor nor the hospital had expressly forbidden them. It was just, Delia suspected, that no one knew what to say. By the time she'd called the police and been carted off to the emergency room, everyone in town must have known about Lindsay James and what he'd done.

A bit awkward, wasn't it? she'd said to herself. One of the members of the fine old families almost murdered by another member of another fine old family. Not acceptable behavior in polite society.

And there was the matter of the other members of still more fine old families who had actually been killed by Lindsay James.

"Feeling better?" Roger asked. He'd been in her hospital room since four A.M., when he'd returned from Nashville. Expecting to wake her with the good news about the race (he'd won first place in two divisions and had trophies to prove it), he'd been met instead with the news that Delia was being stitched up in Jesus Creek Medical Center. Delia wasn't certain how long it had taken him to get there, but she'd known when he arrived. Even inside that sterile emergency treatment room, she'd heard the screech of his tires when he stopped. That had been followed immediately by the sound of Roger's deep voice, bellowing at some poor nurse. ("Get the hell out of my way. Where's Delia?") She loved it.

"I feel great," she said honestly. "What matter a few bruises and stitches and a splitting headache now?"

"Glad to hear that," Reb said. He'd just popped in the door, carrying a small bouquet of flowers.

"Hope you don't mind, Shelton," he said, putting the vase down on her bedside table.

"Not at all," Roger replied, with a wide sweep of his arm.

Reb looked at the floral offering he'd brought, then over at the giant plant on the windowsill.

"Eliza," Delia explained. "The note says, 'Thinking of you.' No doubt. Have you talked to her?"

Reb nodded. "If Lindsay James weren't such a little . . . well, I'd feel sorry for him. Eliza came down to the hospital, of course, soon as she heard. She kept asking him what had happened, as if he was ten years old. Sarah Elizabeth told her to shut up, and she told Lindsay James the same thing. Told him not to say a word. Thanks to Sarah Elizabeth, that Indian lawyer from west Tennessee is already on his way here. Lucky for Lindsay James he married the girl, too. I swear, Delia, I don't think Eliza even understands what's happened. She just acts like Lindsay James got caught stealing milk crates."

"Sure she does," Roger said. He stood up and stretched. "She understands that the family name is mush."

Reb nodded. "I suppose you're right, Shelton."

"Lindsay James is going to be all right, then?" Delia asked. Now that the moment of terror had passed, she could hardly believe it had happened. The only mental picture of Lindsay James that she could conjure was one of the quiet, studious boy she'd taught years ago.

"Physically. Probably his lawyer will try to get him off on an insanity plea. I always figured anybody who commits murder is crazy. Don't know why

that qualifies 'em for anything." Reb looked around
the room as if wondering whether to sit or stand.

There was the rattle of a gurney being rolled
down the hall, then two orderlies maneuvered it
into Delia's room. "Miz Cannon," one of them said
with false heartiness. "You're gonna have a new
roommate."

Delia raised her head to see what was going on.
Reb and Roger had both flattened themselves
against the wall to make room for the new patient's
gurney and attendants. "Miss Constance?" she
asked, convinced that some drug she'd been given
was causing hallucinations.

"That's right," said one of the orderlies. "Miss
Constance had a little stroke last night, didn't you,
darling?"

Miss Constance, looking gray and withered
against the crisp sheets, nodded.

"Spent the whole darned night layin' on the floor,
didn't you, darling?" The orderly seemed inde-
cently intimate with Miss Constance. "No heat on.
Soiled herself, too, like it always happens with
these cases. Good thing a neighbor missed her this
morning or she might never have got help."

Delia waited until they had Miss Constance settled into the second bed, then asked, "How are you
feeling, Miss Constance?"

"A damn sight better than I did last night," the
old woman said. One side of her mouth drooped and
the words were indistinct, but the spirit was there.

"Well, we can recuperate together, then," Delia
said. The exaggerated cheerfulness of the hospital
staff seemed to have rubbed off on her.

One of the orderlies leaned over Delia and whispered, "Miss Constance won't be getting better,

honey. Not at her age. After she leaves here, they'll have to take her on to the nursing home." He picked up the sheet that had covered Miss Constance on the gurney, folded it over his arm, and left, with his partner behind him.

"You like gin rummy, Delia?" Miss Constance asked. "We can pass the time with cards. Why, I could play all night and day."

Delia looked up at Roger and Reb. She knew that they were all thinking the same thing.

"I'll be going," Reb said quietly. "If there's anything you need, Delia, you just let me know."

"Bring us some cards, Reb," Miss Constance ordered. "And some Jack Daniel's. It ain't a card game without Jack. How'd you get here, Delia? Never mind. Let me see if I can guess. Broke your leg on an icy sidewalk, right?"

"Thanks, Reb. I'm fine," Delia replied. "No, Miss Constance, I—"

"Cut yourself peeling potatoes?"

"No, Miss Constance. It's a long story. Lindsay James—"

"Heard he was here. Always was a puny child. I'd recommend some turpentine in a spoonful of sugar. You ever try that for building up the blood?"

Roger moved closer and took Delia's hand. "You feeling okay, babe? Need anything for pain?"

Delia looked over at Miss Constance. "No," she said. "I doubt they have anything strong enough."

ABOUT THE AUTHOR

DEBORAH ADAMS is an award-winning poet, short-story writer, and journalist. Actively involved with Sisters in Crime, the Appalachian Writers' Association, and other writers' organizations, Ms. Adams lives in Waverly, Tennessee. ALL THE CRAZY WINTERS is her second novel, the sequel to ALL THE GREAT PRETENDERS.